Holiday for Inspector West

John Creasey's books have sold nearly a
hundred million copies and have been translated
into 28 languages.

Born in 1908, John Creasey had a home in
Arizona, USA, since more of his books were
sold in the United States than in any other
country. He had another home in Wiltshire,
England, and virtually commuted between the
two.

John Creasey travelled extensively and was
very interested in politics. He was founder
of The All Party Alliance and fought four
elections for this movement, advocating
government by the best men from all parties
and independents. Married three times, he
had three sons. John Creasey died in June 1973.

Holiday for Inspector West

John Creasey

CORONET BOOKS
Hodder Paperbacks Ltd., London

Printed and bound in Great Britain for Coronet Books,
Hodder Paperbacks Ltd., St. Paul's House, Warwick Lane,
London, EC4P 4AH, by Cox & Wyman Limited, London,
Reading and Fakenham

ISBN 0 340 18603 8

Chapter One

JANET WEST kept an eye on her elder son, who was Martin called Scoopy, she amused Richard called Richard, who was sitting on a travelling rug spread over the sands, and she looked for her husband, who had been away for half an hour on a quest for ice-cream.

Martin called Scoopy, who was just two years old, stood watching a tiny girl whose fair, curly hair was half-hidden by a white linen hat. A warm, slanting sun beat down upon the sands and the rippling sea. In Scoopy's hand was a small bucket of water. Suddenly, he raised it determinedly, and Janet called quickly:

"Scoopy, no!"

He sent her a sidelong glance and then allowed a few drops of water to fall on the little girl's feet, turned away from the child and caught sight of a piece of bright green seaweed. While he examined it, Richard let forth a sound between a crow of delight and a cry of pain. Janet looked towards the promenade, caught a glimpse of Roger, her husband, and out of the corner of her eye saw a yellow thing hovering about Richard's curly head. This yellow visitor greatly intrigued one-year-old Richard.

"Oh!" exclaimed Janet, waving the wasp away.

Richard's shrill cry was a measure of his protest, and Scoopy, taking a brotherly interest, toddled up from the water's edge and dangled the seaweed in his face.

Roger West, who was taller than most of the people in sight, came carrying a paper bag gingerly. Bronzed after four days of lazing in the sun, his fair hair still damp from a bathe, in spite of a pair of baggy flannels and a fraying white shirt open at the neck, he was a striking figure.

"Evening News, Member of Parliament murdered!"

5

piped a newsvendor on the promenade behind him. "Murder of a n'M.P., paper!"

Roger stopped abruptly, and Janet sighed. An elderly woman sitting nearby said sympathetically:

"You have got your hands full, haven't you?"

Janet smiled. "Yes, I suppose I have."

"But you've two lovely children," said the woman, "and that makes up for a whole lot, doesn't it?"

"It's everything," agreed Janet. "They're both dears. They—Scoopy! Oh, you little devil!"

Martin called Scoopy, momentarily unobserved, had swung his bucket into the sea, half-filling it with water, and sand and seaweed. He slung the contents at the little girl; the bucket slipped. It fell on the victim's toes, and the scream which rose up drowned every sound nearby, until a woman declared spitefully:

"What a beastly little boy!"

Janet glanced round angrily, but could not tell who had spoken. Scoopy came slowly towards her to face the music, his thumb in his mouth. Janet scrambled to her feet, and the friendly woman said:

"Oh, don't smack him!"

There was no power in Janet's smack, but Scoopy yelled and Richard began to cry and the little girl's screams started afresh.

Into this pandemonium ambled Inspector Roger West, of New Scotland Yard. The paper bag in his left hand was wet and messy, and he was reading the Evening News.

"Roger, for goodness' sake, help me!" cried Janet.

"Eh?" said Roger, looking up from the paper. "Why, what's the trouble?"

With swift joy, Scoopy and his erstwhile victim began to kick at the water which swirled about their feet. Richard was waving a piece of biscuit round and round, and gurgling. Janet was red in the face, ruffled and untidy. Her dark hair had slipped out of her bathing cap on one side, and the straps of her bathing-suit had become twisted. Getting up, she trod on Scoopy's pail, and nearly fell. Roger laughed at her, until he saw that she was nearly in tears.

"Did you have to stay away for nearly an hour looking for ice-cream?" demanded Janet. "And did you have to buy a newspaper and tread on everyone's feet because you were so anxious to read it? I thought we were on holiday."

"And we are!" declared Roger. "Look here, ice-cream! Scoopy!"

A melting, creamy mess from the paper bag was scooped out, put into several saucers and quickly devoured.

Casually, Roger picked up the newspaper.

Janet looked round and saw him reading. She frowned, made as if to speak, but stopped when she saw that he was deeply absorbed. He read for some time, then put the paper down and stared at the sea.

"Come back, darling," Janet said.

He started, and smiled.

"Where did the paper take you?" Janet asked.

"Up to town," said Roger. "Let's forget it, and have a quick dip."

Roger was already slipping off his flannels; he wore his swim-suit underneath. They ran into the water, knee-deep, waist-deep, and then plunged. They swam out a few yards, turning and splashing about. The beach seemed a surprisingly long way off, and Janet glanced repeatedly towards it. Then Roger noticed a floating board, a little farther out, and said:

"Race you!"

He swam well, but over short distances she was faster, and Janet reached the board a little in front of him. It was not large enough for them to sit on, but they clung to it, Janet gasping, Roger smiling.

They started back slowly, doing an overarm stroke, facing each other.

"Darling," said Janet, at the top of a stroke.

"Hm-hm?"

"What did you read in the News?"

"Nothing—forget it."

"I know that—" Janet broke off as a wave splashed into her face—"look on your face," she added, at last. "Absolute absorption. What was it?"

"A murder, if you must know."

"Can't you forget—you're Inspector Roger West?"

"Sometimes," Roger said. "Sorry, darling."

They reached their hotel at a quarter to six. There, Roger dealt with Scoopy and Janet looked after Richard, and by half-past six both children were in their cots.

Roger and Janet went to their room, next door, and emerged in time for dinner sharp at 7.30.

"Now your holiday really begins," Roger said. "Will one of the maids keep an eye on the infants, do you think? I managed to get tickets for the dance of the early season."

Janet's eyes lit up. "Bless you!" she exclaimed. "I'll love it."

They finished a tango, rather breathless, and returned to their table to find a heavily-built man standing by it.

"I hope I'm not making a mistake," said the newcomer, "but aren't you Chief Inspector West?"

Roger said: "I hoped no one would tumble to it down here."

"Oh, I shan't spread it around," the stranger assured them. "I'm Superintendent Kell. Local," he added, and smiled at Janet. "I know you Yard people like to steer clear of shop during a holiday, but I couldn't resist introducing myself to your husband, Mrs West. He sets us all by the ears from time to time, you know."

Janet laughed. "He is rather spectacular."

"Here come!" protested Roger.

"Mrs West isn't far out," said Kell. "Look here, would

you care to join my party? They know who you are, but they dislike shop as much as I do."

Kell's was a mixed party of eight, five men and three women, and Kell was the oldest of them all, a man of about fifty. When Roger and he were sitting alone together at the table, and the rest of the party was dancing, Kell asked:

"What do you make of the Riddel business, West?"

Roger smiled. "I don't know much about it, but I read the story in the Evening News."

"It's on your beat, isn't it?"

"If I were on duty I'd probably be detailed to it," Roger admitted, "and between ourselves I wish I could go back to Town, but I daren't suggest it. This is our first real holiday for years."

"Pity," said Kell. "I mean, a pity you can't get back to Town. It isn't often anyone gets a chance of finding out who killed a Member of Parliament. Did you know Riddel?"

"Slightly."

"Nasty piece of work, wasn't he?" asked Kell.

"Some people thought so," said Roger.

"They made a thorough job of him," said Kell, fingering his bristly moustache. "Beat his face until it was almost unrecognizable and then pretty well severed his head from his body. I bet there'll be some sparks flying before this job is over. Riddel was on some select committees, wasn't he?"

"I only know what I've read," Roger assured him. The music stopped, and he took out cigarettes. "Mum's the word, I don't want my wife to think I'm hankering after the office. We've ten days to go yet."

"It wouldn't surprise me if you're recalled," Kell remarked. They stood up as Janet and Kell's son a tall, amiable youngster, joined them.

The dance finished a little after midnight; Kell offered to run Roger and Janet back to the hotel, but they preferred to walk. A bright moon seemed to dim the lights of the town, and as they walked along the promenade the mellow light gleamed on the water, and the gentle lapping of the sea on the shore was like a distant minstrel chorus.

Janet said suddenly:

"Darling, why didn't you tell me about Riddel?"

"I'm on holiday," answered Roger, lightly. "What ass told you about it to-night?"

"Young Kell. Didn't Riddel ask the Yard for protection? You told me something about it one night."

"Yes," said Roger, "but there are plenty at the Yard to get on with this little job. They'll move everything to find the murderer quickly. Chatworth will be tearing out what little hair he's got, and I'd be for it if I weren't down here. I'm a bit worried about Bill Sloan though."

Janet was startled. "Is Bill concerned?"

"He took over from me for the fortnight," said Roger.

As they reached their bedroom, Roger heard the telephone bell ringing. He hurried downstairs. The telephone was in a recess in the wall of the entrance hall.

"Hallo, Mayview Hotel."

"I have a personal call for Mr Roger West," said the operator. "Is Mr West available, please?"

"Speaking." So it had come.

"Hold on, please." There was a pause, and Roger speculated on the identity of the caller. He wasn't surprised when he recognized Detective Inspector William Sloan's voice.

"I say, Handsome, I hope I didn't get you out of bed," said Sloan, anxiously. "I wanted to get through earlier, but I've had the very devil of a day."

"I was afraid of that."

"Do you think you could come up to Town for an hour or two in the morning? The other beggars are so full of rejoicing because I've slipped up that I hate the thought of asking them for help."

"I'll have to make my peace with Janet, first," said Roger. "Still for the sake of your blue eyes, she'll probably say yes. It will have to be unofficial, though, if I come to the Yard they'll keep me there."

"I'll meet you at Bell Street," said Sloan, gratefully. "Let's say eleven o'clock."

"Right. Has anything turned up?"

"It looked as if we'd get our man after a couple of hours, but complications started to pour in, and—still, this had better wait until the morning. Do tell Janet how sorry I am, old man."

"Well, that's finished this holiday," said Janet, a few minutes later. "I felt it in my bones. It won't be much fun here without you."

"I'll be back in time for the afternoon session to-morrow!"

"I don't think," said Janet, and added resignedly: "Oh, I suppose I'll have to make the best of it."

Chapter Two

A DETECTIVE IN THE DOLDRUMS

ROGER went to London by train, leaving the car for Janet. In the corner of a first-class compartment, he settled down with the morning papers. They had varying accounts of the murder of Riddel, but all of them reported that Scotland Yard expected "important developments" at any moment.

Two men sitting in opposite corners began to discuss the murder. One, fat and opulent-looking, echoed Kell's words.

"By all accounts he was a nasty piece of work."

"These politicians," said the other scornfully. "The man was a carpet-bagger of the worst type. With the money he'd got, he would never have joined Labour if he hadn't wanted a Government post. Damned glad he didn't get it."

"Fellow might have been sincere," murmured the first man.

"Not Riddel," declared the other. "Take my word for it, he was in politics for what he could get out of them. Look at his wife!"

"Well, what about her?"

"My dear fellow, she's the daughter of Lord Plomley, a die-hard Tory. You can't convince me that Riddel would have married into that family if he'd had an ounce of sincerity. Funny thing, that marriage. I could never understand Plomley consenting to it."

"Perhaps he didn't," said the first speaker. "Daughters don't do as they're told, you know."

The fat man picked up his Times and gave it close attention.

Roger sat back, recalling all that he knew of Jonathan Riddel who was returned for a Midland constituency at the General Election, only a few months after he had married lovely Cynthia Plomley. The wedding had caused quite a flutter in society circles. A wealthy man who had inherited most of his money from an uncle, Riddel was always in the public eye, a fact which contributed to the many rumours concerning him. He was said to be a tyrannical employer, mean and greedy.

Roger had seen him when he had come to Scotland Yard to ask for protection. Riddel had been haughty but informative. He said he had received three threatening letters, crudely written notes, all unsigned. A few years before he had charged a chauffeur with theft, and the man had been sent to prison. Riddel had been convinced that this man was the writer of the letters, but nothing had been discovered.

"What was his name?" mused Roger. "Finn, yes, Finn."

A short, thick-set man with a shock of black hair and a

bluish jowl, Finn had then been working in a London factory. He had denied all knowledge of the letters.

Less than two hours after leaving Bognor, Roger was put down by a taxi outside his house in Bell Street, Chelsea. The lawn wanted cutting; he had not had time to do it before he had left. "Might be able to get that in this morning," he thought. "I'll have a shot." He unlocked the front door, and wrinkled his nose. "It's fusty already. Hallo, a letter."

He picked up the solitary envelope. It was unstamped and in the top left-hand corner were the words: "By hand. Urgent and Important." He opened it quickly.

Jonathan Riddel had written to him.

Dear West,
I shall be coming to see you this evening, at 7.30. Please make a point of being in. I do not wish to call at Scotland Yard, for reasons which I shall give you when I see you. This is extremely important. I have reason to believe that an attempt will be made on my life during the next two or three days.

Surprise that Riddel had written to his private address was secondary to the fact that the man had feared an imminent attack on his life, and had made a personal appeal. Had Roger been at home, he might have prevented the tragedy.

He heard footsteps on the pathway, and got up as a man called out:

"Are you there, Mr West?"

"Oh, lord!" muttered Roger. The caller was their next-door neighbour, a middle-aged man named Norman. Roger hid his exasperation and hurried to the front door. "Hallo, there!" he said, heartily.

In Norman's hand was a half-pint bottle of milk. He came into the hall, a diffident little man with a pale, placid face.

"My wife saw you come in. She knows how you like your tea! What a shame you had to come back, Mr West. I suppose it's something to do with that burglary."

"What burglary?" asked Roger, blankly.

"Why, haven't you heard? My goodness, we did have a scare! I should have thought they would have told you, although there wasn't any time for anything to be taken."

"I'd like to hear more of this," Roger said. "Come into the kitchen and have a cup of tea with me."

"Well, I won't say no." Norman trotted ahead to the kitchen. "I am surprised you haven't been told about the burglary, Mr West. It was Monday night. Mr Riddel called, and soon afterwards——"

Roger said slowly: "Steady, now. I'm going round in circles. Do you say Mr Riddel called here and that there was a burglary—in this house—the same night?"

"That's just what *did* happen," said Norman, nervously. "I had thought of telephoning Scotland Yard about it, just to remind them, but I assumed they knew. I mean, they would be informed of anything that happened to Mr Riddel, wouldn't they?"

"They ought to be," said Roger.

Patiently, he unravelled Norman's story.

Just before half-past seven on the Monday evening, a man had come to Roger's house. Norman had been busy in his garden, and had called out to tell him that Roger was away. He had not recognized Riddel then, but Riddel had introduced himself—haughtily, Roger gathered—and demanded Roger's address. Norman had told him that he had not left his address, except with Scotland Yard, but had some difficulty in convincing Riddel that this was true. Then Mrs Norman had appeared, invited Riddel into their house and, perhaps because he hoped to get the address, he had accepted. They had all gone into the Norman's front room, and from there Norman had seen a man enter Roger's garden. Norman had hurried out to tell the newcomer that the Wests were away, but could not see him.

"And then I saw that your front window was open," said Norman. "It was astonishing, Mr West, the man hadn't been there for five minutes. He must have gone straight to the window and forced it up. I didn't lose much time, I can tell you! I shouted an alarm, and Mr Riddel hurried out to help me. I climbed in at the window, and my wife went to telephone the police, and then Mr Riddel followed me. There was a man inside, we heard him although we didn't see him then, but we caught a glimpse of him as he climbed over the back garden wall."

"I see," said Roger, heavily.

"I quite expected you to know about it," Norman went on, "because a policeman came up almost immediately— Mabel didn't have to telephone the police-station, she saw him passing the window and called out. It was quite exciting while it lasted. You see now why I thought you might have come back—because the burglary probably had something to do with poor Riddel's unhappy end."

Roger said: "I'll be after them for not telling me what happened here."

"Perhaps they didn't want to disturb your holiday," suggested Norman. "Well, I must go. Oh, Mabel told me to tell you not to hesitate to come in for some lunch, if you're still here at lunch-time."

Roger thanked him, saw him to the door, and went back to the kitchen, leaving the front door open. He looked in every room, but found no signs of the burglary.

He got out the lawn-mower and started to cut the front lawn, and he had nearly finished when a car drew up.

Bill Sloan got out. "Hallo, Roger! Sorry I'm late."

He was a younger man than Roger, and had only recently been promoted to the rank of Detective Inspector. He was florid with a homely face brightened by flashing white teeth and grey eyes; he shook hands heartily.

"How's Janet and——"

"Fine. Let's get to business," said Roger.

"That suits me," said Sloan. "I knew there would be trouble, but didn't think Chatworth would round on me as he did. Anyone would have thought that I'd been watching Riddel myself."

"Who was?" asked Roger.

"Young Hamilton," Sloan told him. "I wouldn't have put him on, but holidays have taken a lot of the older men away. Hamilton is usually pretty reliable, so I gave him the job. He sent in some good reports, too, up to Sunday night. Then he lost Riddel. He says that Riddel dodged him. Chatworth just won't believe it."

"But Riddel was killed in his own flat. If Hamilton lost him, he ought to have gone back to the flat."

"He was there an hour after the murder," said Sloan. "Or at least, an hour after the approximate time it was committed. The door was open, so he looked in and found—well, you know what he found."

"Are the newspaper accounts pretty accurate?"

"About the discovery of the body, yes. A man from the A.P. was on the spot soon after Hamilton. He said he had an appointment with Riddel, found the door open and walked in, just as Hamilton had done. You couldn't expect him to do anything but rush off with the story," went on Sloan. "Chatworth sent a memo to the Press as soon as he heard of that—the usual tosh about expecting an arrest at any time."

"He'll cool down. What exactly does he blame you for?"

"Putting a youngster on a job of that kind," said Sloan, "and, of course, for not telling him before the newspapers got hold of it. Hamilton telephoned me from the flat and, like a fool, I went straight over before reporting to Chatworth. He read about it in the Evening News. Now he's put Abbot in charge. I never did like that cold slab. He goes about looking as if I've ruined the Yard, and keeps bellyaching about lack of initiative. He's probably given Chatworth a pretty black report."

"Early this afternoon you can go and tell him one or two things that initiative has done for you," Roger said.

"Meaning what?"

"I think you'll find that a man in police uniform but without authority for wearing it came down Bell Street, Chelsea on Monday evening, a little after 7.30. That was just after Riddel had called here to see me and was disappointed because I was away, and after an unknown man had broken into this room and presumably——"

"What the dickens are you talking about?" demanded Sloan. "Riddel came to see you *here*? No one reported any burglary, the newspapers would have got hold of it. You're fooling."

"I'm telling you how you can polish up the tarnished laurels! All you have to do is to talk to my next-door neighbour, and Chatworth will be purring like a contented cat."

"How soon can I see this neighbour?" demanded Sloan.

They went next door, and found Norman only too eager to talk.

Mrs Norman gave them lunch, before Sloan drove off to Scotland Yard. Roger went back to finish off the lawn. At half-past two, when he knew that the boys would have had their midday meal, he telephoned Bognor. Janet answered.

"Well, are you coming back?" Janet asked.

"I doubt whether I shall arrive until this evening."

"Here it comes," said Janet. "Why did I marry a policeman? Have you seen Bill?"

"Yes, and I sent him away cheerful," said Roger. "I'll be back some time to-night and give you a full report. How was it on the beach this morning?"

Five minutes afterwards he rang off. He was torn in two; now that he was in London, the appeal of Bognor,

Janet and the boys was almost irresistible, but once the Assistant Commissioner knew that he had become involved there would almost certainly be a summons.

Just before three o'clock, the telephone rang.

"Here it comes," groaned Roger, echoing Janet, and lifted the receiver. "Hallo?"

A woman said: "May I speak to Inspector West, please?"

"Who is that speaking?"

"My name is Riddel," said the woman. "Mrs Jonathan Riddel."

Chapter Three

MRS JONATHAN RIDDEL

MRS RIDDEL wanted to see him urgently; would he be in at four o'clock? Roger said that he would.

At five past four he began to get anxious; he had felt certain that the dead man's wife would be punctual. He strolled into the garden, and was standing at the gate when a Pathfinder turned into the road, with a woman at the wheel. She stopped outside Roger's house, and got out.

"Are you Inspector West?"

"Yes."

"It is very good of you to see me," said Mrs Riddel.

She was not beautiful, but cleverly made-up. She moved gracefully and with dignity which gave her a great distinction. She was nearly as tall as Roger, slim, with a nice figure. She was wearing a navy blue dress with spotted collar and cuffs. Roger knew that she was thirty-one; she did not look more than twenty-five.

He stood aside for her to enter the cool sitting-room, then offered her cigarettes.

"No, thank you," she said. "I rarely smoke. Mr West," she went on, "I must apologize for coming here. I realize that I ought not to try to get in touch with a police-officer except through Scotland Yard."

"There's no reason why you shouldn't come to see me, Mrs Riddel, but there are limits to what I can do as a private citizen."

"I want very little," she said. "When my husband came to see you the other night, did he bring anything with him?"

"What do you mean by anything?"

She said slowly: "A small parcel, about the size of a flat tin of fifty cigarettes. Did he bring it?"

"I don't know."

"Please don't hedge, Mr West. If you tell me that you cannot divulge information, I will not bother you again."

"I'm not hedging. Your husband didn't see me the other evening."

"*What?*"

"I was away from home."

She said: "It is incredible! He told me that he had seen you. I can't understand why he should have said that if it were not true. He—he formed a high opinion of you, and was anxious to see you personally, I know. It is—incredible!" she repeated, blankly.

"Isn't it all incredible?"

She raised her hands. "I don't know. I have been living in such anxiety for so long that little would surprise me, but this——" she broke off.

"Have you been frightened, too?"

"I don't know whether that is the word." She was more composed now. "I knew that Jonathan was afraid of Finn, but I never believed that there was any real reason for his fear."

"Did you know Finn?"

"I knew him years ago." She sat for a moment, looking at Roger without attempting to conceal her bewilderment, and then she stood up quickly. "There is no point in staying any longer."

"What was in the package, Mrs Riddel?"

"It was something of a private nature."

"Anything of a private nature belonging to him is now a matter of interest to the police," Roger said.

After a long pause, she said quietly: "I don't know what was in it."

"I see. How did you know that your husband intended to come to see me?"

"I have already said that he told me he had been."

"But is that true?" asked Roger.

Colour rushed to her cheeks, and Roger stood smiling faintly. She opened her lips to speak, closed them again, and turned away.

"I resent that implication very much, Mr West."

"I don't like making implications," said Roger, "but I have had a long experience of murder inquiries, Mrs Riddel. I think you will be well-advised to listen to me when I say that the truth nearly always comes out. It can be smothered for a long time, but doesn't often improve by keeping."

"You are impertinent," she said.

"I am a policeman, Mrs Riddel."

She turned towards the front door. He opened it, and Mrs Riddel inclined her head and went out, without looking round. She fumbled twice with the self-starter, then she drove off.

Roger went in, dialled Whitehall 1212, and asked for Sloan; Sloan was with the Assistant Commissioner.

"All right," said Roger, "put me through to Inspector Day."

After a long delay, another voice came on the line—one with a strong Cockney accent.

"Chief Inspector Day speaking."

"Good afternoon, Chief Inspector," said Roger. "This is Chief Inspector West——"

"Who?" demanded Day, his voice squeaking. "Handsome?"

"Yes. I——"

"What's it like down in Bognor, Handsome?" asked
Day, eagerly. "Coo, strewth, it's warm up here. Swelter-
ing. You're a lucky dog, getting a week of weather like
this, but you always do have the luck. How's the wife?
And the family? Done any bathing yet? I'd live in the
water if I was you."

"Eddie, this is urgent——"

"I can't understand a fellow like you, I really can't,"
declared Eddie Day. "You get a fortnight off in the best
part of the year, and then you can't keep away from the
telephone. I'd bury myself a hundred miles from anywhere if I was you, and I wouldn't look at a telephone and
I certainly wouldn't put a call through here. I'll bet Mrs
West wouldn't approve, if she knew you was worrying
about work. Anyone would think," went on Eddie,
spiritedly, "that you imagine we can't get along without
you. We don't do so badly, don't forget that."

"I won't," promised Roger. "Give Sloan a message as
soon as he is free, will you?"

"What is it?"

"Tell him I think he might find Mrs Riddel interesting."

"So you are trying to run the office from Bognor,"
sniffed Eddie. "If I was Sloan, I wouldn't take any notice
of you. Not that he will," he went on, lowering his voice.
"There hasn't half been a do here, Handsome. Poor old
Sloan caught it right in the neck. I happened to be passing
the old boy's office when Sloan was there."

"Will you give him that message?"

"Oh, all right," said Eddie. "You needn't shout. And
I don't suppose it's anything new, he probably thought of
the woman himself. He may have slipped up this time
but he's all right, he won't miss anything. I——" Eddie
broke off, and Roger heard an expression which sounded
like "Strewth!" There was a mutter of voices, but Roger
could not catch the words, until Eddie said in a tone of

disgust: "Hold on, Handsome, here is Sloan. Grinning all over his face. I give up, I really do. Give my regards to the wife."

"Hallo, Roger!" came Sloan's voice. "Want me?"

"How did it go?"

Sloan laughed. "It couldn't have been better! You certainly managed——"

"Don't forget Eddie Day's long ears."

"Well, it went off very well," amended Sloan.

"Here's something else which might go off as well," said Roger. "I had a visit from Riddel's wife this afternoon. Have you seen her yet?"

"She's a pretty cool customer," Sloan told him. "She was out of town the night before last, you know, and certainly wasn't anywhere near the flat, if that's what you're thinking."

"She says that Riddel brought a parcel about the size of a flat tin of fifty cigarettes when he came here, and she also says that he told her he'd seen me. Either he was lying to her, or she was lying to me. She's extremely interested in that packet, although she told me she didn't know what it contained. I shouldn't tackle her about the packet just yet, but don't let her get away with anything. If she puts on airs, try the heavy hand. It'll scare her, even if it doesn't make her talk freely."

"Right!" said Sloan briskly. "I wish you were back, Roger; this is just your job."

"Don't be an ass. Chatworth doesn't know you've seen me, does he?"

"He made a crack about you basking on the sands, but he didn't say anything about sending for you."

"Hold him off, if you can," Roger said. "I'd like to see this week out at Bognor."

He rang off, and went into the hall. The A.B.C. was in the hatstand drawer, and he looked up the fast trains to Bognor. He could catch the next one if he left in twenty minutes. He went round the house, shutting the windows, and drawing the curtains.

He was about to go out of the house, when the telephone rang. "Hold on, please," said the operator, "I've a long distance call for you." She went off the line, but he heard her say: "Hallo, Bognor. I've got your Chelsea number."

Sir Guy Chatworth was a large man, rubicund and rotund of face, ample of girth and, in normal times, genial by temperament. He sat in his large office amid tubular steel furniture and a black, shiny desk, and spoke into the telephone. The sun, reflected from a picture on the side wall, picked up on his bald patch: his hair was grey and curly and grew in tufts at the side of his head.

"Yes, yes, Janet, I know," he said. "It's most trying, I'm really sorry, but you know how important these things are. If young Roger weren't so good I wouldn't have to worry him now, and I thought I would have a word with you first, to soften the blow. How's my godson, by the way?"

"It's not fair, Sir Guy, and you know it isn't."

"Oh, come," protested Chatworth. "This is a cause celebre if ever there's been one! Roger will have the chance of a lifetime. If he distinguishes himself, he'll be made. He ought to be grateful—and you ought to be grateful, Janet. Members of Parliament don't get murdered every day of the week, you know."

"I knew he oughtn't to have gone to Town," Janet said.

"What did you say?"

"I said that I knew he oughtn't to have gone to Town," Janet repeated. "Can't you spare him for another day or two? It's such glorious weather."

"Oh, a day or two. Hum, I don't know, my dear, I don't quite know how quickly this affair will develop, you know. I will promise you this: as soon as the case is finished he shall have this holiday, and——"

"Perhaps you'll arrange an hotel for us, and also command the weather."

"I'll even try and do that," promised Chatworth.

"I—I hope I haven't been too abrupt," said Janet, "it is a disappointment, but I do understand. I hope——"

"My dear Janet, don't worry about that," boomed Chatworth. "I don't mind admitting that I felt guilty when I thought of it. Don't blame Roger, I didn't know he was in London. Look after Scoopy and get as brown as a berry. Oh, where is Roger staying, by the way?"

Janet said hastily: "Well, he might be on his way back to Bognor."

"He'd better not be," said Chatworth. "Good-bye!"

Hardly had he rung off before Janet was putting in a call to the Chelsea house.

Roger was smiling when he rang off; if Chatworth wanted him on the case, it was a measure of his own reputation.

Chatworth would probably ring through at any moment. The telephone bell rang, and Roger hurried to answer. It was the Yard. Through a narrow gap in the curtains he saw Mrs Riddel's Riley draw up outside the house.

Chapter Four

RETURN VISIT

"I would like to speak to Inspector West," said Chatworth, in a voice loaded with sarcasm. "Ask him if he will be good enough to come to the telephone, please."

"West speaking." Roger carried the telephone as far from the table as it would go, then leaned forward with hand outstretched, to try to move the curtains so that he could get a wider view. The car door slammed.

Mrs Riddel was approaching the house, and Roger was impressed again by her unusual grace.

"This is the Assistant Commissioner," announced Chatworth.

"Oh, hallo, sir," said Roger, brightly. "Will you hold on just a moment? There's someone at the door."

He put the receiver down and hurried to the hall. The sound of the bell still echoed faintly. He opened the door and said: "Come in and sit down, please, I won't be long. Help yourself to a cigarette and a drink from the table."

He picked up the telephone again. "Sorry about that, sir."

"I want to see you at once, West," Chatworth growled.

"Oh lor," said Roger.

"What have you against that?"

"I promised my wife I would catch the next train."

"I'm sorry, West," said Chatworth, and put down the receiver. Roger went into the living-room.

"I'm glad to see you again." he told Mrs Riddel, as he lit a cigarette for her. "We're reasonable people, you know. Our job doesn't always make us popular because it turns us into Paul Prys, but few people have any real reason to complain about the way we treat them."

"Do you always use this prologue when talking to witnesses?" she asked.

"Whenever there seems to be a risk of misunderstanding, yes!"

For the first time, he won a smile. Mrs Riddel tapped the ash from her cigarette, stood up, and began to move about the room.

"I hope there won't be any misunderstanding, Inspector. My second thoughts seemed best. The contents of that small packet were of great interest and importance to me and to my husband, but I do not think they will be of any interest to you. The packet has now been found."

"That's good," murmured Roger.

"Perhaps you would like to look at it."

"I would, very much."

She opened her flat red bag, took out a packet wrapped in brown paper and handed it to him.

"I have already broken the seals, to make sure that the contents are intact."

"Thank you." Roger took off the paper wrapping, and dropped it into the chair behind him, a casual action which she did not appear to notice. In his hands was a case of black moroccan leather, with gold hasp and gold hinges. He examined it closely, then opened it.

Inside on black velvet was an exquisite pearl necklace, with two rows of pearls perfectly matched and graduated in the case, in the shape of a double heart.

Roger looked up.

"You must be very glad to have these back, Mrs Riddel. Were they stolen from your husband?"

"No. They were found, after all, in a suit-case. I only thought they had been stolen."

Roger's eyes gleamed. "And you came to me for them."

Unexpectedly she laughed. "I mean that I thought they had been stolen when I did not find them here. My husband told me on the telephone on Sunday evening that he was going to bring them to you, because he did not think they were safe in his keeping. You will ask why he did not take them to his bank or to a safe-deposit." She shrugged. "I cannot answer that, Inspector. I cannot explain any of my husband's actions in the last few weeks, except that he was living under a great strain, and did many things which must have appeared eccentric."

Roger paused, and then asked deliberately:

"Do you think he was murdered for these pearls?"

"I have no idea." Her coolness was quite remarkable. "Do they seem to you a sufficient motive?"

"Yes," said Roger, "but I doubt whether such a savage murder would have been committed if robbery had been the motive. Thieves and murderers are usually opposites, you know. The attack was of such a brutal nature that——"

"Inspector, must you be so detailed?"

"What a thoughtless fool I am!" Roger snapped the jewel-case shut, and handed it to her. "Thank you very much for letting me see these. And for explaining a mystery which might have taken a great deal of time to clear up." She stood up, and he went with her to the door.

He glanced at the brown paper on the chair. Apparently she had forgotten it, and she put the jewel-case into her bag. "There's just one other thing I ought to say," went on Roger, "and that is—visits to a policeman's private house are apt to be misunderstood. I might be suspected of collusion. I can always arrange to see you privately at Scotland Yard."

"I doubt whether there will be another occasion for me to see you privately," replied Mrs Riddel. "I hope there will be no unpleasant consequences after my indiscretion this time."

"Oh, once doesn't matter!" They reached her car. "Goodbye, Mrs Riddel, and thank you very much!" For the first time they shook hands. Her hand was very cool, and she had a firm grip. With her hand on the gear-lever, she looked round at him and said abruptly:

"Do you know who murdered my husband?"

"Not yet," said Roger. "We shall find out."

"I will help you in every way I can," she promised.

Further along the road, a small two-seater sports car turned into the King's Road a few yards ahead of the Riley. Driving it was a young detective officer: Sloan had lost no time in having Mrs Riddel watched.

"Well, we're moving," Roger said aloud, "and Bill's right—she's pretty cool."

He went upstairs and came down with a small attaché case. Handling the brown wrapping paper with extreme care, he folded it and put it into the case. Then he picked up his cigarette-case from the table on which Mrs Riddel had placed it, wrapped it in a clean handkerchief, and laid that in too. He left the house, went by bus to Westminster Bridge and hurried to the Yard. He did not go immediately to Chatworth's office, but went first to the finger-print room, where a pale-faced man sat with a watch-maker's glass on a high stool. On the bench in front of him were dozens of articles, bottles, handbags, boxes, spoons in remarkable variety, some valuable, some cheap.

"Hallo, Joe," said Roger. "On duty to-day?"

Joe put his head on one side, and squinted up.

"No, I'm on holiday, like you."

Roger grinned. "Then do a rush job like me." He took out the brown paper and the cigarette case. "Run over these for prints, will you? There will be a roar from Chatworth in about a quarter of an hour, and he'll want results right away."

"He always wants results right away," grumbled Joe. "All right, Handsome, I'll look 'em over."

"Thanks." Roger went out and made his way to his own office, on the first floor.

There were four yellow desks in the room, with sections partitioned off at the back of each, marked: In, Out, Wait-Attention, Rush and Special. There were no papers in any of these sections on one of the desks. The others were littered but none of the Chief Inspectors who shared the office was in. He unlocked his desk, and looked up as the door opened.

Chief Inspector Eddie Day came portentously into the office, looking suspiciously at Roger. He was a tall man, his waist-line was large, but his head and feet were small, so that he appeared to taper off at either end. His well-tailored suit was a greenish-grey, which drew attention to his figure. His thick grey hair was brushed straight back from his receding forehead. He had a pointed nose and prominent teeth, which showed even when his mouth was closed. No one who saw him for the first time could believe that Eddie Day had the intelligence to be a high official at Scotland Yard. Those who knew him well barely tolerated him, but had a great respect for his skill in detecting forgery. There was no one in England to touch him on his particular subject.

"Well, I'll go to Bedlam!" he said, in his Cockney twang. "So you've actually come back. I suppose you had a special request from the Lord High Commissioner, I don't think."

"That's the solemn truth," declared Roger. "He's waiting for me now."

Eddie said: "You beat the band! Anyone would think there wasn't another detective in the building. That's what comes of crawling," he added with a sniff. "'Adn't you better be off?" He invariably dropped his aitches in moments of stress. "You'd better not keep 'im waiting."

"Oh, I can get away with anything," declared Roger airily. "You've had another go at those anonymous letters Riddel received, I suppose."

"Been through 'em three times because Chatworth wouldn't believe me the first time," said Eddie. "My report's just the same now as it was when I first looked at them. Written by someone with a good flowing hand who tried to diguise it. Nine chances to one that a woman wrote them, and it certainly wasn't the man Finn."

"That's good enough for me," said Roger. "Thanks, Eddie."

He went along to Chatworth's office, knocked and entered. Chatworth was sitting with his hands flat on the desk before him, his big head a little on one side.

"It's so nice of you to come, Inspector West," he said ironically. "Sit down . . . I suppose you want me to apologize for disturbing your holiday."

"I'm very glad to be on duty," said Roger.

"All right, let's hear what you've got up your sleeve," said Chatworth.

Roger talked . . .

After ten minutes, Chatworth picked up a telephone, called finger-prints, and said: "Forbes, have you finished working on the brown paper which Inspector West brought in just now? . . . Bring it along at once please."

Joe Forbes arrived promptly, and delivered his findings in a flat, monotonous voice.

"Paper covered with prints, sir. Mostly a lady's, we've got no record of them, so it's no one who's been through our hands. The only other prints were Mr West's, and there weren't many of them. Two or three of the same lady's prints were on the cigarette-case, the rest were Mr West's."

Chatworth said: "What cigarette-case is that?"

"Mine," said Roger, and took the case back. "Mrs Riddel handled it. Well, we know she brought a dummy packet, sir. The original would have had Riddel's prints on it as well."

"All right, Forbes," said Chatworth, and when Forbes had gone: "You'll concentrate on the lady, and don't let her fool you."

"We'll watch her, sir."

"Good! And get this case over as soon as you can. Superintendent Abbott will be in charge, but he'll work here. Sloan will be with you, and you can call on as many men as you want. The fact that Riddel was a Member of Parliament means that it will have more publicity than any case we've handled for years. The Press will be hounding us, the Home Office will be prodding us—in fact, they've started—and a question's been asked in the House about it. We can't afford to fail or waste time. There is, too, the fact that Riddel was doing special Government work, on a Committee. Did you know that?"

"I've no details," Roger said.

Chatworth went on: "Here are the bald facts. A Government committee has been set up to inquire into the workings of certain combines and trusts. There were rumours that some of these were evading the new company regulations. Lord Plomley is on the Board of Directors of one of the trusts which is being investigated. Riddel's wife is Plomley's third daughter. None of this had become public knowledge yet, but it almost certainly will soon. It has the makings of a first-class scandal. One obvious theory is that Riddel discovered some tricky business in the Plomley Trust, and threatened disclosure. By that, I mean that he gave his father-in-law warning that the disclosure would be made, and so was murdered. The fact that his wife is behaving mysteriously lends colour to that theory."

Roger said: "There are the other members of the Committee, they'll know as much as Riddel did."

"They all say they know nothing," said Chatworth. "The Home Secretary tells me that they've no knowledge of anything along those lines. It was a committee of five originally." He opened a manilla folder on his desk and pushed it across to Roger. "There are the names. Riley hasn't sat on it, he was taken ill soon after it was formed, so there are three left—Marriott, Garner, Henby. It isn't reasonable to imagine that three Members of Parliament would conspire to conceal information, but you might get something from them. Your first job had better be to interview each one. They know they'll be hearing from us, and I think you'll find them helpful. But mind how you go, and keep me fully informed."

"Of course, sir. Riddel's anxiety started about the same time as his work on the committee?"

"It began about a month afterwards. The committee has now been sitting for more than three months. It's a complicated business and even without this interruption would have gone on for some time."

"Are the other M.P.s being watched?"

"Yes, since this morning."

"Did Sloan know?"

"I doubt it. Abbott detailed the men for that. Sloan hasn't covered himself with glory, you know."

"We can hardly expect him to do a good job if some of the moves are being kept from him," Roger said. "I may take him into my confidence."

"I shall leave that to you," said Chatworth, and then waved an admonishing finger. "But you can't take anyone else into your confidence. I know your friend Mark Lessing often likes to give you the benefit of his advice, but he mustn't have any inside information this time. Now, I've got to be off," added Chatworth, abruptly. "I've several engagements to-night. Good luck."

"Thank you, sir."

He went out, turning over the fresh information in his mind, and hoping that Eddie Day had gone home. He would be able to think more clearly if Eddie were not interrupting continually. Roger relaxed in an arm-chair usually kept for visitors, but he had hardly settled down before the door burst open.

He looked round, and saw Superintendent Abbott. It was unlike Abbott to do anything in a hurry; as a rule he sidled into a room, his face pale and his eyes dull. Now there was a tinge of colour on his cheeks, and his eyes were blazing.

"Hal-lo!" exclaimed Roger, jumping up.

"Where's the Assistant Commissioner?"

"He's gone home," answered Roger. "What's the trouble?"

Abbott said: "Marriott's been shot. Marriott is another of the members of Riddel's committee."

"Killed?" demanded Roger, sharply.

"No, but in a dangerous condition. I must telephone the Assistant Commissioner." Abbott went to the telephone. "I think you had better go to the hospital, West, and find out when Marriott's likely to come round."

"I'll send someone else," Roger said, already at the door. "I'd better see the other members of the committee."

Chapter Five

MESSRS GARNER AND HENBY

COLONEL RANDOLPH GARNER was the only Conservative M.P. who had served on Riddel's committee. Roger knew of him but had never met him. A man widely respected on all sides of the House, he had been an active back-bencher during the days of the Coalition Government, and was one of the most constructive critics of the present Administrations. He was wealthy, and his house in Grosvenor Place was one of the minor social Meccas of London.

Roger waited in the long hall for five minutes, and was growing impatient when the footman who had admitted him came in quietly.

"Will you come this way, sir?"

"Thanks," said Roger, and followed the man up the stairs and across a landing. Their footsteps were muffled by the thick fitted carpet.

"Ah, come in, Inspector," said Garner, rising from a large pedestal desk. He shook hands. "Sit down. You needn't tell me why you've come, of course. What will you have?"

"Nothing, thanks," said Roger.

"Oh, you must have a drink," insisted Garner. "There's no need to stand on ceremony here, you know. Whisky and soda?"

"Well—thanks."

There was whisky, a syphon and glasses on a tray on the

desk. The room was lined with books, and had the look of being much lived-in. The arms of the easy hide chairs were rather shabby and there were faded patches in the carpet. The desk itself was leather-covered, and rubbed in places. In spite of that, there was an atmosphere of luxury and well-being in the room.

Garner was a short, dapper man, faultlessly dressed in a dinner-jacket. One electric light on the desk glistened on his starched shirt-front and pearl studs; the pearls reminded Roger of Mrs Riddel's second visit. Garner's plentiful hair was almost white and was brushed back from his forehead.

"Here's luck on your job," he said, raising his glass. "You've got your hands full, Inspector! It's a miserable, unhappy business. I knew Mr Riddel fairly well, you know. Liked him very much. Pay no attention to the rumours which were spread about him. He was a poor mixer, of course, but an admirable fellow. His death has shocked all his friends."

"I'm sure it has," murmured Roger.

"It seems such a senseless business," went on Garner. "I suppose the only possible motive was burglary, although nothing appears to have been stolen. A senseless murder must be more difficult to deal with than any other; I don't envy you in the next week or two. But I expect you've formed one or two theories, haven't you? Ready to be knocked down when another one turns up!"

Roger said: "We haven't even got as far as theorizing yet, sir. We shall need a lot more information before we can do that. Personally, I'm much more worried about another aspect of the case."

Garner stared at him; he had keen grey eyes, and, in spite of his talkativeness, he gave the impression of being a man who was naturally calm.

"That's an odd thing to say," he observed.

"Well, sir, with Mr Marriott now a victim——"

Garner dropped his glass. It struck the edge of the desk and broke, spilling the whisky over the carpet. Roger did not move; Garner's face was drained of colour, and the earlier impression of remarkable composure disappeared; he was obviously frightened; badly frightened.

"Are you—sure?" He ignored the broken glass and the whisky, but took a cigarette from a box on the desk; his hands were unsteady.

"I'm afraid so," said Roger.

"How—how did it happen?"

"He was shot as he got out of the car to enter his club," said Roger, who had spent a few minutes with Sloan before leaving the Yard. "He's now being operated on at the Westminster Hospital, and his chances aren't too good."

"I had the impression that Riddel was a badly worried man," said Garner. "I imagined that he had some personal troubles, but he never discussed them with me. So Riddel's murder wasn't exactly a surprise," Garner went on, beginning to talk too quickly. "It was a shock, but not a surprise—somehow it seemed to fit in with his anxiety, his general secretiveness during the last few weeks. But Marriott—that's a very different matter. Why, I saw him only this afternoon. He was in the best of spirits. You say he was shot while getting out of his car to go into his club?"

"Yes."

"Good God!" exclaimed Garner. "What a shocking thing. I—but have you caught his assailant?"

"Not yet."

"You must get him!" cried Garner. "Good God, man, you shouldn't have let a murderer get away in broad daylight—wasn't Marriott being watched by the police?"

"Yes."

"It doesn't reflect much credit on you," declared Garner. "The very fact that you arranged for Marriott and me to be watched proves that your men were on the look-out for such an attack, and yet you let them get away with it. You must do better than that."

"We will," said Roger grimly. "Have you any reason to think that you might be attacked, Colonel Garner?"

"After Marriott, I don't know what to think," said Garner, "I really don't know what to think." He finished his second whisky, and stubbed out his cigarette. "I hope I can rely on more efficient protection."

"That will need co-operation from you, sir," answered Roger.

"I'll help—of course I'll help," promised Garner, and gave a little nervous laugh. "There can't be any reason why a man should want to shoot me, but I shall feel much safer when you've got the maniac under lock and key. Er—what kind of help do you want?"

"Detective-Sergeant Deacon is waiting outside, sir," said Roger. "I would like you to give him a list of your engagements and probable movements during the next few days, and tell him if there are likely to be any alterations in it. There will be two men from headquarters here, very soon, and they will watch the house day and night. I don't think you need worry," Roger added, getting up.

Roger had Deacon brought up and introduced, then excused himself and drove to Lambeth, where Henby lived. It looked as though Garner did consider himself to be in danger, and that he thought the attack on Marriott had brought that danger nearer. Roger could not rid himself of the impression that Garner had put on a bold front when he had first entered the room, and that he had something to hide.

Roger pulled up outside a house half-way along a street leading from Lambeth Road. There were only four houses standing in the block, all that was left of a long terrace. The rest had been destroyed during the fires in 1942, and not yet rebuilt.

Outside Henby's, the end house, was a detective-officer who came up at once as he recognized Roger.

"Hallo, Gill," said Roger. "Any trouble here?"

"None at all, sir." Sergeant Gill was an experienced and cautious officer. "Mr Henby's been in for the last two hours."

"Any visitors?"

"No, sir, no one's been near the place. One or two of the other gentlemen who live here have come in and out, sir."

"Thanks," said Roger. "You'll have reinforcements and relief soon. Mr Marriott's been shot," he added, and as he went towards the front door, Gill gaped. The door was open. On the wall immediately inside the hall was a notice-board, and on the board were pinned several cards.

The house was divided into flatlets, and was occupied by several Members of Parliament who had not been able to find more suitable accommodation. All of them were Labour M.P.s. Roger had read a report on Henby's domestic arrangements before he had left the Yard. An oldish couple did the main cooking for these M.P.s, all of whom were back-benchers, youngish men who, with the exception of George Henby, had never been in the House of Commons before.

No one appeared as Roger walked along the passage. The house needed repairs but was clean. He went up the creaking stairs to Flat 4, where Henby lived, and paused outside the door when he heard the murmur of voices. Someone laughed.

Roger knocked on the door. There was a momentary pause before the door opened and George Henby stood there. Roger recognized the M.P. from photographs which had been in the files of the Riddel case. Henby was a tall, good-looking man of nearly forty. He had won a by-election shortly before the last general election.

"Good-evening," he said, and then looked at Roger's card. "Oh, police." He gave an attractive grin. "Come in. Charlie, the police have found us out at last! Inspector West, Mr Charles Ingleton."

Ingleton was younger than Henby, a chubby little man dressed in crumpled clothes. Henby wore a pair of carefully creased flannels, and an open-necked shirt, which emphasized his lean figure.

"You won't want me here," said Ingleton, "and I've got to go, anyhow." He waved to Roger. "Good hunting!" he said, and went out.

Henby pointed to a Windsor arm-chair.

"Well, how can I help you?"

Roger glanced about the room. On one side there was a huge glass-fronted book-case, crammed with books, and in a corner was a roll-top desk; the pigeon-holes were tidy and the desk itself was clear except for one sheaf of papers and a colume of Hansard. There was nothing else in the room worthy of attention.

"Getting the atmosphere?" asked Henby cheerfully. "That's the proper thing to do, isn't it? I suppose poor Marriott's bad luck has brought you along."

"News travels fast," said Roger formally.

"And this piece will travel faster than most," replied Henby dryly. "When Ingleton told me—he'd just come in agog with the news—it gave me a nasty jolt. This committee seems fated. The sharpshooter got away, didn't he?"

"Yes," said Roger.

"You people are having a rough deal, and the hounds will be on you pretty fast," said Henby. "Sympathies, and all that kind of thing." There was an undercurrent of seriousness beneath his flippancy, and it came to the surface with his next words. "It's a pretty shocking business, West, and I wish I could help. I can only tell you that Riddel was in a poor state of nerves for the last few weeks. In fact, it started before that, but it's only been noticeable lately. I've got my ideas about the reason for it, but you're not interested in the ideas of a humble M.P., are you?"

"I'm interested in anything to do with Riddel and Marriott," said Roger.

"Not to be used in evidence against me?"

Roger was cautious. "If you want to give me some information in confidence, it will stay confidential unless it has a direct bearing on the case."

"I don't think Riddel was happy in his domestic life," said Henby. "In fact, I'm sure he wasn't. He told me so, on the only occasion that I've ever known him drunk. He didn't say much, but it was enough to tell me that he doubted his wife's—er—affections."

"Do you mean that she was having an affair?"

"Must you reduce everything to the lowest common denominator?" demanded Henby. "That is what I gathered Riddel thought. I know her slightly. I'm not a bit sure that I should have told you anything about this, but if it might help——"

"We would have discovered it sooner or later," Roger assured him, "and knowing now might save Mrs Riddel some unpleasantness. You needn't reproach yourself.

"There is something else," Roger went on. "Put down on paper everything you remember about Riddel's nervousness. Days when he showed any special signs of being uneasy, and that kind of thing. It might help a great deal."

"Not easy, but I'll do it," promised Henby.

"Thanks. Are you nervous yourself?"

Henby raised his eyebrows. "Nervous of being shot at, you mean, or being knocked about like Riddel? No, I'm not nervous. I've been used to taking care of myself. If you mean, have I any reason to think that these people will now have a shot at me, no, I haven't. Nothing turned up in our investigations to give anyone a motive for killing us—not as far as I know, of course. There is one other little thing——" he broke off, eyeing Roger speculatively.

"I had a telephone call from Riddel on the Monday morning," he said. "I only recalled it this afternoon. He told me that he was very anxious to have a few words with me, and asked if I were free that morning. As it happened, I'd a deputation from my constituency waiting for me, and I couldn't get rid of them too quickly. I told Riddel so, and he said that later would do, and rang off. I don't know whether it means anything, but I thought you would be interested."

A sharp tap at the door cut across his words.

Roger had heard no sound of approach, but he remembered the way the stairs had creaked as he had walked up, and he looked hard at the door. Henby went towards it, but Roger said:

"Let me open it, will you?" He stepped in front of Henby, who looked at him in surprise, opened the door and then quickly stood aside. He caught a glimpse of the man standing there, and laughed at his own groundless fears. "Hallo, Gill," he said, "you didn't make much noise!" It was the man who had been watching the block.

"No, sir," said Gill, softly. "Don't make a sound, sir." He slipped inside the room with a furtive movement, and closed the door. "A man has just broken into the house. He's next door now, I think—at least, he went in at that window."

"*What?*" demanded Henby.

"No noise, please," pleaded Gill. "Someone stopped me and asked directions, I think he was trying to distract my attention. I could see the house in the window of the room opposite, though, and watched the man climbing up. Then this fellow went off, and I saw a pair of legs disappearing into the window of the next room to this. Shall I send for help, sir?"

Chapter Six

CAPTURE

"I THINK we'll tackle this on our own," said Roger. "Go downstairs, Gill, and keep your eyes on the window."

"Right, sir, but——" Gill hesitated.

"What's worrying you?"

"I don't think the man who asked me for directions went far," said Gill. "He might come back if there's any trouble, and I thought we ought to have more on the job than you and me."

"What's the matter with me?" asked Henby.

"Well, sir, we can't ask you to——" began Gill.

"Nonsense!" declared Henby. "And Ingleton will lend a hand if you think we need a fourth, West."

"I think we'll manage," Roger said. "Stay close to the house, Gill, and call out if you see this fellow coming back. Those reinforcements I told you about might be here any minute."

Gill nodded, and went off. Henby was trying to repress his excitement. Roger waited until Gill had gone quietly downstairs, and then opened the door again.

"What do we do?" whispered Henby.

"Barge in," said Roger. "Whose room is it next door?"

"My bedroom," said Henby.

"Locked?"

"The key's on the inside."

Roger nodded, and stepped softly to the door. The quiet inside the house was broken by the wail of a tug's siren on the river. Roger turned the handle, and pushed gently. The door was locked. The wail of the siren continued, and Roger was grateful for anything which helped to muffle the sounds he made.

"Shoulders to it?" queried Henby.

"Is there any other way into the house?"

"There's the back door, of course," Henby whispered. "Why?"

"I want to know which way he can run," said Roger. "It's a flimsy-looking door," he added, in a voice pitched so low that Henby could hardly hear. "We'll have a shot at it."

"Right!"

They stood side by side, leaned back, and then launched their combined weight against the door. There was an ominous creaking noise, but it held. They tried again, but it still held.

"It's blocked," said Roger, and then called out in a normal voice: "Open up, there!"

They could hear movements in the room, as if someone were in a great hurry. No one spoke. Henby thrust his weight against the door again, but without any result.

"We need a crowbar," he said, ruefully. "We can't let the beggar get away!"

"He won't get away," Roger said. "I hoped to catch him on the hop, but we won't do that, either." There was a new sound inside the room. "He banged against the window, so he's on his way out. Stay here, will you?"

As Roger turned to hurry down the stairs, Ingleton came out of the room opposite. He said something which Roger did not catch as he joined Henby. Roger was half-way down the stairs when Gill shouted from the street; by the time Roger reached the front door Gill was out of sight. Roger turned left, towards the windows of Henby's room, and as he reached the corner of the house he saw Gill standing a few yards away from the wall, peering up intently. He saw Roger and waved him to silence.

A little man was climbing from the window. He supported himself against the window-sill and a drain-pipe, shinned down without any fuss, and did not once look behind him. He jumped the last few feet, straightened up, and turned.

"That'll do," said Roger.

Fear swept the man's face. He darted towards the left, but Gill stretched out a hand and grabbed his coat. He wrenched himself free and tried the other direction, but Roger blocked his path. He crouched against the wall, his hands held in front to ward them off, and he began to breathe heavily.

"You haven't got a chance," reasoned Roger. "Don't ____"

The man launched himself at them, his arms lashing out. He took the other two by surprise, and Gill went down from a back-handed blow which caught him on the side of the face. The man's other hand just touched Roger, but Roger swayed aside in time to avoid the full force. He could not stop the little man from breaking clear, or from running fast towards the street. Roger turned, shouting: "*Stop him!*" The little man was bewilderingly fast, and turned left, towards Lambeth Road. Roger dug his elbows into his side as he raced after him. The fugitive was gaining a little. Roger put on a burst, made up a few feet, but could not keep that pace up. Gill was now pounding behind him, and the children playing on the heap of rubble were watching, gleefully.

Roger heard the voices but did not hear what the boys were saying. They were fifty yards from the main road, and the little man was ten yards ahead of them. Once in the main road, the chances would be fifty-fifty; the man might be able to lose himself in the crowd, or his progress be stopped long enough to let Roger catch up.

Then, from the other side, one of the boys darted forward. There was a yell of protest from the others, but the boy ignored it and rushed straight at Roger's quarry. He flung himselff orward in a low tackle. The fugitive had no idea of what was about to happen, and crashed down.

Roger could not slow down in time to avoid him, but made a flying leap over him. When he turned round several of the boys were cuffing the lad who had so effectively turned the tables on the runaway, and Gill was trying to separate the boys and at the same time to keep an eye on the little man.

"That's enough!" Roger called, and the boys stopped, but muttered among themselves. Roger put his hand into his pocket. "Have you got any silver, Gill?" asked Roger, glacing at the coins in his hand. "Give the little chap five shillings and the others half a crown apiece, and get their names and addresses."

"Yes, sir," said Gill.

Roger gave him what silver he had, and turned to the captive. The man had been badly shaken by the fall, and was now trying to get up. Roger helped him. He sat on a low wall and wiped the perspiration off his forehead. There was a nasty graze on his right cheek and the skin was rubbed off his nose, but neither wound was bleeding much.

Roger took the man's wrist. He led him, unprotesting, back towards the house. The boys were now crowding round Gill, who was taking their names and addresses before parting with any money. Henby and Ingleton came hurrying from the doorway.

"Nice work!" congratulated Henby.

"Don't congratulate me," said Roger. "The boys back there collared him for me." He pushed his captive into the hall, and up the stairs. The man was docile enough now, and sat down heavily in the Windsor chair in Henby's living-room. Henby and Ingleton stood by, watching eagerly.

Roger went through the man's coat pockets. A tattered wallet yielded several dog-eared letters, all of which were addressed to Mr Bert Bray, or B. Bray Esq. Roger put them on the table together with the other oddments,

none of which was of interest, and asked casually as Gill
came in,

"What were you doing next door, Bray?"

Bray stared at him, and muttered: "N-nothing."

"Now don't be a fool. What did you come for?"

"N-n-nothing!"

"You'd better come clean, nothing can help you now but
the truth. Why did you break into Mr Henby's room?"

Bray said sullenly: "I'm not talking."

Roger said: "Look after him, Gill, and see what you can
get out of him."

He led Henby and Ingleton out of the room and into
the bedroom, the door of which was now open.

"A chair was lodged against it," Henby told him. "We
managed to get it open a few inches and move the chair.
There doesn't seem anything wrong."

"Did you keep anything of value in here?"

"No, everything that matters is in the other room."

"Do you mind looking in the drawers while I give the
bed a once-over?"

"For what?" asked Ingleton.

"He didn't come here for nothing," reasoned Roger.
"If there was nothing to take away, there might have been
something to leave behind him."

He folded the bedspread over the foot-rail, did the
same with a blanket and sheet. Henby was half-heartedly
going through the drawers, but Ingleton was not even
pretending to be interested in anything but Roger. When
the bed was stripped, Roger asked:

"Lend a hand, will you?"

They each took a corner of the mattress and rolled
it back; there was nothing between it and the springs.
They let it drop back and started at the other end. Suddenly Ingleton exclaimed:

"Well, I'm damned!"

"What's that?" asked Henby, sharply.

"Look!" cried Ingleton. He darted forward, his hand outstretched.

"Don't touch!" snapped Roger.

Ingleton pulled his hand back, as if stung. Roger laughed at his expression, adding: "There might be fingerprints, you know, and you could smear them."

He stood looking at a small brown-paper parcel. Henby brushed the hair out of his eyes, peered at the parcel and then looked hard at Roger.

"Have you ever seen this before?" asked Roger.

"Yes," said Henby.

"Where?"

"On Riddel's desk," answered Henby. "It was there when I went to see him on Sunday morning. At least, it was one very much like it," he added, peering more closely. "It's fastened with gummed tape and I remember it was dented at one corner, like that is. Did you expect to find that here?"

"I expected Bray to have left something behind."

"Aren't you going to open it?" Ingleton asked.

"I shall have to do that at headquarters," Roger said. "If you care to come along, Mr Henby, you can be present when the deed is done."

"Thanks," said Henby. "Any chance for my friend?" There was an irrepressible sense of humour in him.

"You can tell him about it afterwards!" Roger tried to put the parcel in his coat pocket, but it was just too large. "Take Bray to Cannon Row, Gill," he ordered, "and take special care of him. Drive immediately behind me," he added, and went downstairs. Except for a few gaping boys there was only a cyclist in the street. Roger glanced at him. Gill bustled Bray into the small police car, while Henby opened the door of his own Vauxhall. Roger went round to the other side, intending to drive, holding the packet in his free hand as he opened the door. As he started to get in, the cyclist passed him.

Next moment he felt the packet snatched from his fingers. He backed out of the car again, but cracked his head on the door-frame. Half-blinded by the pain, he could only just see the cyclist pedalling furiously along the road.

But the cyclist had reached the corner and was out of sight before either of the cars moved off.

Chapter Seven

MORE ABOUT BRAY

REALIZING that he was not steady enough to drive, Roger stopped his car almost as soon as it had started. The other car was already turning the corner. Ingleton and two policemen in uniform were standing on the kerb by the house, Ingleton muttering something which Roger could not hear.

"Are you all right, West?" Henby asked.

"I shall be in a moment," Roger muttered.

"You'd better have a drink," said Henby.

Ingleton led Roger upstairs and back into Henby's sitting-room. Ingleton went into his own room and came out again almost immediately with a half-bottle of whisky and a syphon.

He mixed a drink.

"Sit down and take it easy," he advised, "and don't imagine that you've met your Waterloo. This is the first time I've really believed in Scotland Yard. I like men who make mistakes and have set-backs occasionally."

"I don't like men who fall asleep on a job." Roger looked grim. "May I use the telephone?" He shifted his chair so that he could reach the instrument, and dialled Whitehall 1212. Abbott came on the line at once. "We've made some progress," said Roger. "We've caught a man named Bert or Herbert or Albert Bray, of 18, Fisher

Street, Lambeth. He's on the way to Cannon Row now. Gill will charge him with breaking into and entering Mr Henby's flat."

"I see." Abbott never showed enthusiasm.

"On the debit side, a small packet which Bray hid in Henby's room was stolen from me by a cyclist about five minutes ago."

"Did you say stolen from *you*?"

"Yes." Roger was brusque. "The cyclist was a young man between the ages of 20 and 25, thin, dark-haired, hatless, dressed in light grey flannels and a brown leather lumber jacket. He was riding a sports model bicycle in excellent condition, but I don't know the make. He turned right into the Lambeth Road towards Westminster Bridge. Is that all clear?"

"Come and see me when you're back, West, please," said Abbott.

"Chilly reception?" asked Henby.

Roger grinned.

"How on earth did you notice all those details?" demanded Ingleton, round-eyed.

"I saw him coming along the street," Roger explained. "With any luck we'll have him before the night's out."

"Look here, West," Henby said, "do you think that packet was up in my room to frame—that's the word, isn't it?—your humble?"

"Yes I do."

"Then it must contain dynamite!"

"I think it does."

"I can't think you're right," piped up Ingleton. "What point would anyone have in popping the packet under Henby's mattress? It could have stayed there for weeks without being discovered."

"The mattress does get turned sometimes," Henby argued.

"Never mind about that." Ingleton was much the more

insistent of the two. "Henby could only have been success-
fully framed if you people had come to search his room,
and you'd hardly do that, would you?"

"A Member of Parliament is not above the law,"
Henby interjected solemnly.

"I know we're not above the law, but West wouldn't
have come barging in here and searching the room just on
suspicion. The packet wouldn't have been found for some
days, and even when it was found the police might never
have heard of it. I mean, if it's incriminating."

"Are you suggesting that it might have been a billet-
doux for me?" Henby, his pipe drawing well, pointed the
stem towards Ingleton.

"I'm just indicating some flaws in West's theory."

"You're a whale for destructive criticism," Henby said
ruefully.

"It isn't destructive, it's constructive, isn't it, West? It
makes you think of other possibilities. Fixed ideas won't
help you, you've had enough experience to know that."
Ingleton was brisk. "I don't think the packet was planted
to incriminate Henby, because of the difficulty of getting
you to search his room. Show me how a man could over-
come that, and I'll withdraw my objections."

"I can't show you yet," admitted Roger.

"There you are," crowed Ingleton.

"Oh, dry up, Charlie," said Henby. "West will get
a poor opinion of the country's governors if you go on like
this. From what I know of him, he wouldn't be above
making a search on any pretext. That's what comes of
getting a reputation for being unorthodox, West!"

"I'm the most orthodox of policemen," Roger assured
him. "But I shall be in bad odour if I don't look in at the
Yard."

"Ten to one you don't catch your cyclist by midnight,"
offered Henby.

"I don't think I'll bet," Roger said.

Henby's remarks interested him. They might have been spontaneous, but there was certainly a chance that he had been fishing for Roger's real opinion.

At the Yard, Abbott was cold and formal. It was a great pity that West had allowed the packet to be stolen. The case was nothing but one unfortunate mistake after another. The only redeeming factor was the arrest of the man Bray.

"And we wouldn't have got him if it hadn't been for a boy not yet in his teens," admitted Roger. "Have you seen Bray?"

"Yes."

"And he's still refusing to talk, is he?" murmured Roger. "What's the latest news of Marriott?"

"The bullet has been removed, but he is still on the danger list," Abbott told him. "Have you made any further progress? The Assistant Commissioner is coming in at half-past nine, and I hope we shall be able to give him a more satisfactory report than we could if he came in now."

"That depends on the cyclist and Bray," said Roger. "I think I'll have a word with Bray." He watched Abbott open a manila folder. "You've been digging into his past, I suppose?"

"Naturally," said Abbott. "You had better study it."

Roger felt depression deepening. The case was more involved than he had realized, the complications were not going to be easily unravelled, and not many Members of Parliament would be as friendly and obliging as Henby. By now, Colonel Garner was probably making strong representations to the Home Office about police inefficiency, and by the morning the attack on the second M.P. would hit the headlines of every newspaper.

He studied the report on Bray.

His record was mediocre and there had been no complaints against him. He had worked variously as a street hawker, a shop assistant and clerk to a bookmaker. He was not on the police records, he was single, and he lived in two rooms in a street in Bethnal Green.

Bray remained sullen, however, but he still manifested tense nervousness, as if too frightened to give information to the police. There was no way of making him talk and, a little before eight o'clock, Roger left with Sloan to search Bray's rooms. A portly woman, neatly dressed, protested when they first arrived, but when they showed their cards and warrants she asked them in. The house was little more than a hovel, but it was well-kept, and Bray's room was tidy. There were a dozen paper-covered books by his bedside, a rather ostentatious radiogram and a pile of gramophone records.

They made a thorough search of the room, even rolling up the square piece of linoleum, but found nothing helpful.

"Another blank." Sloan was worried. "When are we going to get anywhere, Roger?"

"To-night, I hope," said Roger, with forced cheerfulness. He went downstairs and talked to the woman, who answered his questions briefly and, he thought, was telling the truth. Bray was a model lodger. He rarely had visitors, in fact he had not received one for over three weeks. He came in regularly to meals, and the only complaint she had about him was his habit of playing his gramophone after midnight; even that, she admitted, might be worse, for its tone was good and not too loud. No, she did not know the name of any of his friends, if he had any friends. He rarely went out for a drink, and when he did it was to a public-house some distance away. Roger noted the name of the pub.

"The story of a blameless life," he said.

"Are you going to have the house watched?" asked Sloan.

"We'll leave that to the Divisional people," Roger said.

"We ought to see them soon. We'll have a word with the Lord Naseby crowd first, I think."

The Lord Naseby was a free house with a good reputation. The landlord was a little man with a huge, almost bald head, and was most anxious to please. Yes, he knew Bray slightly, a very nice, quiet fellow who came in about twice a week. Sometimes he was on his own and sometimes he had a girl with him. No, the landlord did not know the girl's name; but the landlord's wife believed Bray had called her Ethel. The landlord's wife also remembered seeing her behind the counter at a nearby popular store; and she distinctly remembered seeing her only the night before in a new, expensive dress. The landlord's wife recalled that clearly because Ethel had been with another fellow, named Tandy.

"Now Tandy's a really nasty bit o' work," said the landlord. "If you was after him it wouldn't surprise me, gents. And he ought to be stopped riding in and out of the traffic the way he does, he nearly knocked the missus down the other night. Didn't he, Lil?"

"Didn't he!" exclaimed Lil. "I'd give him fancy riding!"

"Motor-cyclist?" asked Roger, with quickening excitement.

"Motor nothing, just a bike," said the landlord. "He's a trick cyclist at fairs and things, and does he fancy himself!"

"Does he!" echoed Lil.

"Where does he live?"

"Down at the Arches," said the landlord, "you know. The old Arches near the river, what they used for air-raid shelters once. Turned one of them into a fancy place, I'm told, but I haven't been there to see for myself. Why, are you after Tandy?"

"Is he sallow, dark, slim, somewhere between twenty-five and thirty——"

"That's him!" cried Lil, "that's him all right, that's Tandy!"

The Arches were at the end of a short, narrow road, and most of the houses in the road were uninhabited. Many were roofless and windowless, and the few which were still occupied were those at the entrance to the street. There were seven or eight arches in all, built for a railway line that was now used only for occasional goods traffic.

All this, Roger and Sloan learned from Superintendent Adams of the A.Z. Division.

Roger had telephoned Divisional Headquarters from the Lord Naseby, and found Adams in the office. He knew the Superintendent well, and was confident that he would leave nothing to chance. Men were on the way to the Arches before Roger reached the police station, where Adams, big and burly, welcomed them with cups of steaming cocoa.

"Any news?" asked Sloan anxiously.

"Give us a chance," protested Adams, "my men have hardly had time to get there yet. What do you want Tandy for?"

"The Riddel business," Roger said.

Adams widened his eyes. "I shouldn't have thought Tandy would mix in high society! We've been keeping an eye on him for some time, mind you, but we haven't got anything on him yet. We think he does a bit of cat-burgling, and gets away on that bike of his. What's the charge?"

Roger explained as they sipped their cocoa, and then the telephone rang. Adams answered it, and immediately his expression hardened, and excitement showed in his eyes. Sloan and Roger stared at him tensely, while he listened and when he said abruptly:

"Yes, stay there. I'll bring help." He replaced the receiver, only to lift it again and say: "Give me Martin—

hallo, Martin. Have four men ready at once for a trip to the Arches. We'll have to break a door down. There's a man giving trouble there and they want him at the Yard." He rang off, and grinned. "Tandy's inside the place and won't come out; he's barricaded the doors. You've found your man all right. Coming?"

Roger drove with Sloan and Adams as passengers, and a Divisional Inspector drove the other car, leading the way through the murky, ill-lighted streets. Roger drove on the brakes, anxious not to lose a second. Soon they turned down a long, wide road not far from the docks, and Adams leaned forward:

"We're nearly there."

The leading car pulled into the side of the road, and Roger stopped immediately behind it. Out of the shadow of the houses a man came hurrying. There was no noise, not even the ordinary noises of the night; the stillness and the quiet were uncanny.

"Nothing's happened," the man repeated.

Adams called his inspector, and gave his orders crisply. He knew the vicinity well, as did his men, and he did not once falter.

They had pulled up a few yards from the end of the narrow turning leading to the Arches, and there was no escape except along that turning. One car was to be driven into the street and the headlights switched on, to illuminate the Arches clearly. Tandy's particular arch was the one immediately opposite the street itself.

Before the car was moved into position, three men walked along the dark street, so that they would be close to the arch, but invisible to the men inside it; they were to break down the doors with crowbars, if necessary. The men went off, dodging in and out of doors to avoid being seen in the light of the two gas-lamps which illuminated the street.

The night was warm, and a mist hid the stars. The

uncanny quiet remained, and was broken only when the police car turned into the street. On went the headlights, and their beam showed up the battered houses and the huge wooden doors of the arch in front of them. There was a small door cut into the big doors, and near it stood one of Adam's men. Two others were stationed a short distance away from him.

Adams, Sloan and Roger walked behind the car and stood by its side, in the darkness. Adams waited until the driver had climbed out, and then put his hands to his mouth. A loud-speaker was superfluous when Adams was about.

"You there, Tandy!" he roared. "Tandy! Listen to me! You can't get out, don't play the fool!"

There was no answer.

"Come out at once!" roared Adams.

Nothing indicated that the arch was occupied, there was no sign of movement, and the quiet seemed more intense when Adams stopped shouting.

"The fool," growled Adams, and then shouted again: "All right, you asked for it!"

The men close to the arch moved in and raised their crowbars. One battered at the large doors, the other two set to work on the smaller one; they intended to force an entrance that way.

"I suppose he's still there?" queried Sloan.

"What's the matter with you tonight?" asked Adams, good-humouredly, "The place has been watched from the moment I sent the men here. There's only this way out, we'll have him in a couple of jiffs. Look, they've nearly got the door open. They——"

He stopped abruptly.

The small door opened without warning, and a powerful jet of water was projected into the street. It caught one of the policemen in the stomach, and he dropped to the floor, squirming. The others, drenched and helpless, staggered back under the full force of the water. Adams, Roger and Sloan made a concerted rush forward, but the jet was turned on them drenching Adams and Sloan, and knocking them over. Roger had a moment's warning, and fell flat on his face, avoiding the full force of the stream. As he did so, the door slammed and the jet stopped.

Adams got up, squeezed water out of his hair, and muttered angrily. As they collected themselves, a small hatch at the top of the big doors opened, and the nozzle of the hosepipe was thrust through and pointed downwards. Water hissed out on to the men who were still near the arch. They did not linger, but came running back to the car. The stream of water followed them; in the garish light of the headlamps there was something ludicrous as well as mortifying about their retreat. They came stumbling and panting past the car, and the jet was switched on to it. Water smacked against the radiator and the windscreen, while the fugitives crowded behind the car, gasping for breath. The only dry spot where they could shelter was immediately behind it, and Adams and Sloan joined them. Roger made a rush towards the porch of one of the battered houses, and, reasonably dry, watched the arch doors. The hissing of the water drowned his voice when he called out:

"They're going to run for it!"

He saw that none of the others heard him, moved out of his shelter and slithered into the next doorway. At the sides of the street the water fell with less force, but the jet was being swept from side to side, keeping the middle of the road under bombardment. The car was drenched; one of the men tried to see what was happening but was struck by the jet of water and bowled off his feet.

Roger was halfway between the car and the arch when he saw the small door open. A man stepped into the roadway, paused, leaned inside, then pulled out a bicycle.

Roger ran into the open. The men at the end of the street,

who could see what was happening, would surely come to help him. He rushed towards Tandy, who actually started to mount his bicycle before he saw Roger. In the glare, Roger saw his mouth open and he shouted, but the hiss of the water from the hosepipe drowned his words. Tandy's dark hair was in his eyes, he looked a little pimp of a man.

He pushed the bicycle against the wall and met Roger's rush. Roger shoved him to one side, Tandy lost his footing on the slippery surface, and Roger grabbed the bicycle. It was unbelievably light. He picked it up with both hands as Tandy rushed at him again, and hurled it as far as he could. It went several yards through the air, crashed down on the handlebars, then fell over.

Tandy reached him and kicked at his legs and stomach, wild with anger. Then another man appeared, grabbed Roger's arm and pulled him inside the arch door. Roger could just hear him bellowing: "Come in, Tandy, come in!" before he was flung to the floor of the poorly lit room, banged his head heavily, and rolled over, hardly conscious of what was happening.

Chapter Eight

THE DEFENCE OF THE ARCHES

WHEN he began to recover, Roger found that the light inside the arch was brighter, and the door was closed. Tandy was leaning against a chair, gasping for breath and glaring. One of the men in the room, a heavily-built fellow, strode to Roger's side, and pulled him up by his coat lapels.

"Let's have a look at you," he said, and then exclaimed: "Strewth! We've got the big fish, it's Handsome West!"

Roger tried to shake himself free.

"Now you be a good little boy, Handsome," said the big

man, with a leer, "we don't want to spoil that pretty face of yours. But we will, if you start anything." He shook his fist in front of Roger's nose. "That's not bad on its own, and with knuckle-dusters it can do quite a job. Gimme them dusters, Sam."

The third man, a pink-faced shrimp of a fellow, took a pair of knuckle-dusters from the table. Tandy did not look at them, but stared at Roger all the time. The big man fitted a fearsome-looking thing over his left hand. It was like a flattened steel bracelet, which covered his knuckles; steel spikes, a quarter of an inch long, stuck out from it. He swung his fist through the air, and laughed.

"Lost your tongue, Handsome?"

"You've lost your head," said Roger.

"So you're awake, are you? Well, listen to me." The man's voice hardened, and he drew nearer, holding the knuckle-duster only a few inches from Roger's chin. "You know what to expect if you try any tricks. Tandy and me are going to escape, see. You're going to tell the tykes out there to hold off, and if you don't your wife won't re-cognize you." He raised his voice, and it rivalled Adams's. "Anything happening, up there?"

Someone called from above their heads:

"They're in a huddle, Benny."

"They'd better stop that way," said the big man. "Come with me, West." He grabbed Roger's arm and hauled him forward.

One side of the arch had been converted, fairly snugly, into living-quarters. On the other side was packed an assortment of oddments. Automatic machines, parts of fair-ground side-shows, several bicycles, all brightly painted, notice boards painted in gay colours, guy-ropes, guy-pins—all the paraphernalia of a fair circus.

There were wooden partitions, which divided the ground floor section into four rooms and, apparently, passages. The big man led Roger into the main passage, cuffing him when his foot caught in a mat and he stumbled.

In front of him was a ladder leading up to a loft.

"Get up there, Handsome, and no tricks."

Roger had to obey. He reached the wooden ceiling, in which there was a hole about a yard square. He hauled himself through this and stood up. The big man put his hands on each side of the hole, to follow.

Roger stamped heavily on the thick fingers. The man snatched his hands away, swearing, as Roger saw a flat expanse of wooden floorboards, with a rough bench and one or two stools but no other furniture. The bright, unshaded bulbs were hanging from the ceiling. At the window a man sat holding the nozzle of the hosepipe, which he was directing on to the street below. The water was switched off but the man did not glance round.

Near the hole was a large square of wood, obviously used to cover the opening. Roger bent to pick it up. He glanced over his shoulder and saw the little man half-way through the hole; the big man was out of sight. Roger dropped the wood with a crash, and ran forward, smacked his fists into the little man and made him fall down the hole.

The man with the hosepipe heard the crash and jumped up. The big man called up from below:

"If you do that again I'll bash your head in." He gasped between every word. "I mean it. Here, Sam, stand aside and let me get at him."

Roger watched the man with the hosepipe as he bent down for the hatch-cover again. In spite of its weight he managed to drop it into position. It caught on two corners, but it would prevent anyone climbing through quickly. He kicked at it, hoping to jam it into place, as the man at the window moved warily towards him.

In his hand was a knife.

Roger saw a marked likeness to Tandy; this man was probably the cyclist's brother. He was taller and more powerful, and he meant business. Roger crouched ready to jump either way. Would the man throw the knife or use it at close quarters?

There was a thump at the hatch-cover; it moved a few inches and dropped down again.

Tandy's brother said: "Lift that cover up."

Roger still did not move.

"Lift that up," repeated Tandy's brother, "or you won't know what's come to you." He was crouching, legs and arms bent, and held the knife behind him, so that Roger could not see it.

There was another thump at the hatch.

"Suit yourself," said Tandy's brother, and threw the knife. It came like an arrow towards Roger's chest. He flung himself sideways, but felt a sharp pain in his right arm, below the elbow. There was a metallic sound as the knife stuck into the wall. Tandy's brother straightened up and hurled himself at Roger. He came over the hatch-cover; as he reached it there was a third thump, and he caught his foot in a corner which poked up. One moment Roger thought that he was finished, the next Tandy's brother was sprawling at his feet, face upwards. Roger bent down, grabbed his head and banged it on the floor.

The hatch-cover rose up a few inches and Roger caught a glimpse of the big man's face. He stamped the cover flat, turned away from it, pulled the knife out of the wooden wall, and ran to the front of the loft where the nozzle of the hosepipe was drawn up through a hole in the floor. Roger gripped this with both hands and hauled it up, the heavy piping spreading snake-like. It was full of water, more than he could easily handle. He put it down and turned to the open window.

He heard Adams's voice.

"We'll burn you out if you don't come!"

Roger leaned out, dazzled by the glare of the head-lights. Two other cars were in the street, now, and policemen were approaching on either side, but they darted into the doorways of the houses as Roger appeared.

He saw Sloan pointing at him.

"Get a move on!" called Roger. He turned, hearing a sound behind him. It was Tandy's brother, crawling towards the hatch. Roger picked up the nozzle, squatted down and, directing the nozzle on the man, cautiously turned the control key. A gentle stream of water rose up and fell half-way between him and the hatch. Roger saw Tandy's brother glaring at him and making a frantic effort to quicken his pace.

The hatch-cover was moving up and down; Roger thought that the men below were using something as a battering ram. He pretended to be in difficulties with the hose, and the stream of water gained little strength. Tandy's brother reached the hatch-cover.

Roger opened the nozzle wider; the jet shot over the other man's head, and the hose seemed to jump and almost wrenched itself out of Roger's hands. He regained control and lowered the direction of the jet. It was so powerful that Tandy's brother was swept aside and driven half-way towards the wall, where he collapsed again. By then the big man's head and shoulders were coming through the hatch. Roger gave him the full force of the jet. He disappeared beneath the sheet of water, and Roger switched off.

He rested the nozzle on the floor and glanced out of the window. The police were still approaching cautiously, when he heard a new sound: the crack of a shot.

One of the policemen nearest the arch fell forward, tried to get up, then fell again. The other attackers disappeared into doorways as if by magic.

There was another shot. This time Roger was listening for it, and knew that it had been fired from the room below. So Tandy and his companions had left shooting to the last; with two guns and a dozen rounds, they could hold out for hours.

Tandy's brother was crawling towards the hatch again; he had guts. His clothes were dripping water, his mouth was open and he was obviously in pain, but he did not stop moving when Roger went towards him. Roger grabbed him by the coat collar, turned him on his back and dragged him towards the hatch. Exerting all his strength he eased and then raised the hatch-cover, moved it aside then dragged his man towards the hole, feet first.

He pushed him down the ladder, as a bullet struck the side of the hatch.

"That's the way, waste 'em," Roger grunted.

Tandy's brother lodged on the ladder. Roger left a corner of the cover off and hurried to the hosepipe, picked up the nozzle and dragged the pipe towards the hatch. By lying face downwards and directing the jet through the hole and towards the big doors, he could prevent further effective shooting in either direction. The thick floorboards were probably proof against the weight of bullets which the defenders were using.

Moving the hosepipe was nothing like as difficult as it had been when he had first tried.

Another bullet struck the side of the hatch. It made him flinch, but he pushed the nozzle into position, then stretched himself out at full length. He took care not to expose any of the pipe itself; a bullet through it could destroy his hopes of out-matching the guns.

He switched the water on at full pressure.

There was one powerful burst, which shot out with a loud hissing noise, and then it stopped and only a trickle of water came from the nozzle.

He stared at it stupidly, turned the tap off and then on again; nothing happened. Only slowly did it dawn on him that they had turned off the water below.

"You'd better give up, West!" That was the big man, his voice very hard. "You won't get out alive if we don't go free. What about it?"

There was no sound for some seconds, not even from the street. Then Benny swore, and the echo of a shot sounded in the arch. Another and another followed.

Roger looked round for a missile, and caught sight of some small blocks of wood in the corner. As he picked them up there was a thud against the wooden doors. Other thuds followed. They were not heavy enough for a battering-ram; it was almost as if someone other than the police was trying to get in. Then there came another, higher up the doors, probably just below the ceiling. Something hit the side of the small window, which Roger had left open. It tumbled inside, and as it fell smoke issued from it.

One moment the brightly lit room was vivid in his eyes, the next it was filled with heavy black smoke, which spread with bewildering speed, and Roger staggered backwards with his hands over his face. The smoke grew thicker and thicker, it was difficult to breathe.

He heard shouts from below, as if they were being smoked out too, then staggered forward, trying desperately to reach the window. He banged into some wall, knocking his forehead and nose. He groped blindly about, and came up against another wall, and began to cough and choke.

The men below were coughing, too, and he could hear their footsteps. Then he heard a thump closer at hand; the hatch was being moved! He heard the men climbing through. They hoped to find more space up here, this emergency had made them forget that smoke rises. Now they were on the same floor as he, he could hear them close to him. They were coughing. Roger tried to repress a cough, to avoid betraying his position, but a spasm shook his whole body and he retched and was sick. He realized with relief that the noise he had made would not necessarily be attributed to him: anybody might cough and retch.

A heavy footstep sounded close behind him.

He moved to one side. The window was now a danger-spot. He managed to stifle another fit of coughing, stepped silently forward, three long steps. The hatch was at least five yards from the front of the arch, so he reckoned there were two yards to go.

"West!" Benny sounded almost at his side.

Roger was getting more used to the smoke. Breathing was easier, and he could think more clearly. He went forward another yard.

"You needn't think you'll get down the hatch," Benny called. "I'm standing by it."

Roger took a step forward, and his foot went into space. He stood on one foot by the side of the hatch, then went down on his knees and reached down with his right foot. He touched one of the rungs of the ladder, then slowly went down.

His foot had just touched the ground floor when something crashed into the wooden doors. The smoke was thinning, and he could see a hazy patch near one of the lights. He went towards it. After a long, tense pause, there was a reverberating crash; the doors had fallen in. Something hit Roger on the leg, the echoes of the crash continued but there were other noises, as if missiles were flying about and hitting the walls. Then he saw lights, misty at first, then brighter, and in the lights the shapes of men. The light fell directly on to one man, and Roger could see he had a gas-mask on.

One of the masked police shone a light on him, and called out:

"Here's one!"

"I'm West," croaked Roger. "West! The others are upstairs. Careful, they're armed. Careful."

Then a strong torch was focused on him, and someone called out in jubilation: "The Inspector's all right, sir!"

"Upstairs," repeated Roger. "Upstairs, be careful!" His voice trailed off.

Chapter Nine

WITNESSES

"Now take it easy, Roger," urged Bill Sloan. "They can't do anything up there, we've smoked them out. Take it easy, old chap. We'll soon have you right."

"I'm all right now," declared Roger. "There's no need to carry me."

In five minutes, after a cup of tea laced with whisky, he was feeling much better. Then he remembered the pain in his arm when Tandy's brother had thrown the knife. Sloan helped him off with his coat. The cut was hardly worth the name, the skin had only just been broken.

"You might find out what's happened along there, Bill," Roger said.

"They'll report in good time," said Sloan.

"I may be impatient, but——"

Footsteps in the hall made Roger break off. Adams was speaking to someone, with unusual deference. "I quite agree, sir. I assure you West is not seriously hurt."

Roger sat up as Chatworth entered the room. He tried to get to his feet. Sloan pushed him down, and Chatworth planted himself in front of his chair and said gruffly:

"I should think so. Do you want to go out on your feet? You sit down, too, Sloan, you look as if you've had a busy time. I hope you're not as bad as you look, West!"

"I'm perfectly all right, sir," Roger assured him. "A wash and brush-up is all I need." He looked at Adams. "How are they getting on at the arches?"

"It's all over," said Adams. "Three alive and one dead."

"Don't worry about what's happened here, West," Chatworth said. "It's been a good night's work."

"I think we ought to start on the little man, sir. He'll talk."

"The little man's dead," Adams told him.

Tandy's brother had been wounded in the shoulder and the head. He was in hospital suffering from concussion. Tandy and Benny were bruised and dazed, but were not badly hurt. Sam the Shrimp had been found at the foot of the ladder with his neck broken.

These things Roger learned as Sloan drove him to the Yard; and then young Hamilton drove him home.

Hamilton was freckled, merry faced, in the middle-twenties, had won early promotion from the uniformed branch. Roger liked what he knew of him. Hamilton was full of the night's events, and laid stress on the fact that Tandy and all the others at the Arches were partners in a small travelling fair. They did not own all the side-shows, but they made the bookings and superintended all the arrangements. They used two of the arches to store their goods. What Hamilton could not understand was why circus people were concerned in the attacks on Members of Parliament.

"At least, I can't make sense out of it," added Hamilton. "Have you picked anything else up, sir?"

Roger grinned. "I've heard people call Parliament a circus; perhaps that's the connection."

There were lights at two or three top floor windows, but only one from a ground floor room; his own.

Roger climbed out of the car, stopped twenty yards from his gateway, and looked back, watching the light and Hamilton walking towards it. Then he went along a narrow path between two houses. There was no light from that side.

He opened the small gate at the side of the garage, using his key, and softly approached the back door. Now that he was closer to the house, he could see a reflected light somewhere inside. His own footsteps sounded loud and distinct on the cement pathway. He reached the back door and turned the handle. The door was locked. He had his keys in his hand, inserted one cautiously, opened the door and went in. He could hear nothing.

He stepped into the passage leading to the front door. The light was coming from the front room, the door of which was not quite closed. He thought he could see the shadow of a man.

The shadow moved.

Roger stood quite still, prepared for trouble. Instead there was a musical clang; the piano was being opened. Next moment someone began to play a Rachmaninoff prelude.

"Well, I'm damned!" Roger grinned.

His close friend Mark Lessing also had a key. Mark, against whose "assistance" Chatworth had already warned him, used the Bell Street house as his second home.

Roger reached the door. He could see the pianist's back; the dark wavy hair proved that he was right. He hesitated for a moment, waited until Mark broke into the quick movement; then he thumped his fist on the door.

Mark shot round on the piano stool.

"Who——"

"Good evening, Mr Lessing," said Roger.

"Go away, you!" said Mark, crossly. "You made my heart jump a mile."

Roger went to the front door, where Hamilton was obviously prepared for anything, but he stepped forward when Roger called out:

"It's a false alarm, Hamilton."

"Oh, that's good sir." In the hall light, Hamilton looked disappointed.

"I don't know that there's going to be much for you to do," went on Roger, "but you'd better stay."

Roger went back to the front room. A tall figure in a well-cut, light grey suit, Lessing stood in front of the mantelpiece.

"Inspector West can now share his troubles," he announced.

"Inspector West has been ordered not to," Roger told him.

"You aren't going to take him at his word, are you?"

"It's a ticklish business," Roger admitted, sitting down and stretching out his legs. "I'm not wide awake enough to talk much to-night, Mark, and even if I were I'd have to sort the wheat from the chaff. I'll tell you all I can."

"And I've inside information, and all that kind of thing." Mark looked glum.

"What kind?" Roger demanded.

"I have a nodding acquaintance with the Riddel family," said Mark, "and I'm not a stranger to the Plomleys. However, if Chatworth's said no——"

"I'll have a word with him in the morning," promised Roger. "I shall be in his good books until then, anyhow. We had quite a time to-night; if you want to hear about it, you'd better come to bed."

They used the spare room, where there were twin beds. Roger did most of the talking.

"I suppose you're telling the truth when you say you know the Plomleys," Roger said.

"I'm not a bosom friend of the family, but I know them," Mark assured him. "I knew Cynthia fairly well, when she was young and gay."

"Cynthia?"

"Riddel's wife."

"Oh, yes."

"She hasn't been gay since she married Riddel."

"Eh?"

"Oh, go to sleep," said Mark, "and give your mental machinery a spot of oil."

"I'm not sleepy now. Was there a change in Cynthia Plomley after she married Riddel?"

"Most decidedly."

"Have you heard anyone else say so?"

"Most of her friends."

"Any special reason for her change of mood, marriage apart?"

"That was for love," replied Mark in a sepulchral voice.

"I thought it was supposed to be. There was no love lost between Riddel and Plomley, was there?"

"No. But it wasn't really a love-match," repeated Mark. "Mind you, I don't know that Cynthia Plomley would have worried about hurting her father's feelings. Independent young woman, in many ways, and in spite of her airs and graces, a thoughtful politician. Conservative, of course, but genuinely progressive. You can imagine how Plomley liked that! I thought Plomley would disown her, about a year ago. She was seeing a lot of a youngish political crowd, some of them nearer Communist even than solid Labour. She and Henby saw a lot of each other. I think it would have been a more suitable match for her than marrying Riddel, but the poor fellow had no money." Mark did not know that Roger was now sitting up in bed, staring through the darkness with increasing interest. "I fancy that Plomley read the Riot Act. Marry Henby and you get cut off with a shilling. Something went wrong, anyhow. Probably she couldn't face life on a few hundreds a year. Henby stopped moving in her circle, and that was that. I—oh! Are you getting out of bed?"

Roger said: "Yes," and switched on the bedside lamp. He reached for the telephone. "I'd forgotten that I promised to tell Henby what luck we had," he added, and dialled Henby's number.

He was thinking of Henby's statement that Riddel's wife was suspected of having an affair. Had Henby given him that information because he wanted to help, or was there another reason?

Chapter Ten

PAST HISTORY

ALTHOUGH it was nearly half-past one, Henby did not keep Roger waiting.

"I hope I didn't get you out of bed," apologized Roger. Henby chuckled. "I wondered whether I would hear from you before the night was out. With an apology, I suppose, for not getting your packet or your cyclist. I wish you'd put money on him! I'm just finishing that report you asked me for, by the way. You ought to be grateful."

"I am," said Roger, "and you would have lost your money."

"What?"

"The cyclist, whose name is Reginald Tandy, is now in jail and will be up before the magistrate in the morning. I can't tell you anything about the packet yet."

"I congratulate you," said Henby. "Is the case nearing its conclusion, or isn't that the right phrase?"

"I'm not sure we've got as far as that yet, but it's a useful step. I thought you might like to know that Marriott has a fighting chance now, too."

"Splendid! Outlook for Henby and Garner, more settled."

"I should think so."

"Well, many thanks for ringing," said Henby. "I can now sleep easy. I say, West, I've a childish hankering for a visit to the holy precincts of Scotland Yard. May I bring these notes over myself in the morning?"

"Yes, of course."

"Thanks, old man. About ten o'clock."

"It will have to be before half-past nine or after midday," Roger told him. "I shall be at Bow Street from ten until eleven-thirtyish."

"Well, I might look in there, too," Henby said, and laughed. "I'm certainly forming a better impression of Scotland Yard! Good night!"

"Good night," said Roger, and rang off. He stretched out for a cigarette, and Mark, now sitting up, struck a match. They both lit up.

"What crazy idea is in your mind now?" asked Mark. "Are you going out?"

"No. Two good men are watching Henby's place, and if he goes out I shall know about it first thing in the morning," said Roger. "I can't think that he's got anything to do with it, though."

"Tell me exactly what you're thinking," said Mark.

"Isn't it obvious? Cynthia Plomley, unable to marry man she loved because of his poverty, married rich man who gets murdered. Cynthia, wealthy in her own right, can now marry whom she pleases. Henby is a promising politician, probably marked out for junior ministerial post before long. He struck me as being pretty sound."

"Henby's clever," said Mark, "and he's got what is badly needed in the House, a sense of humour. He takes life seriously but not sombrely. But I shouldn't present Chatworth with that theory, if I were you. It might not be well-received, and to suspect Cynthia Riddel of murder——"

"I didn't suggest that," objected Roger. "I merely remarked her husband was conveniently murdered. Now I'm going to sleep. Goo'night."

Bow Street was crowded. The Press was there in strength, and many people were standing. Henby, who had not called at the Yard before half-past nine, was near the door; Tubby Ingleton was with him. Roger, looking round the court-room as he went into the witness-box, wondered if he would see Cynthia Riddel, but she was not there. Sir Leonard Brayle, senior partner in Messrs.

Brayle, Longley, Brayle and Brayle, solicitors, was surprisingly in court, being treated deferentially by one of the ushers. Brayle was rarely in a police court and certainly he was not watching the interests of any of the accused. They were represented by a keen young solicitor from the East End.

Details of Bray's burglary, the theft of the packet and the affair at the Arches were given briefly and with as little colour as police witnesses could manage. Benny—whose name was Harrison—and Reginald Tandy were charged and remanded, at Roger's request, for eight days.

Roger went below, to attend to the formalities, and when he got upstairs he found that Mark and Henby were talking together, but Ingleton had gone. Henby looked in high spirits, but Mark was saying very little. Roger joined them, and Henby patted him on the shoulder.

"Well done, West! I've been telling Lessing that I've been eating humble pie all the morning."

"That'll do you good," said Mark.

"A prophet has no honour in his own country," smiled Henby.

He gave Roger a sealed envelope, and they got into Roger's car. At the Yard, Roger spent a few minutes in his office; he was not surprised to hear from Eddie Day that Chatworth had asked to see him as soon as he returned from Bow Street. Roger called up the A.C., who said:

"Ah, I've been waiting for you. Will you come along?"

"May I postpone coming for a quarter of an hour, sir?" asked Roger. "I've got a man with me whom I think is worth a little attention."

"All right, but don't make it longer," said Chatworth. "Who is it?"

"Thank you very much," said Roger blandly. "I'll be along sooner if possible."

He hurried out to the waiting-room, where Henby

and Mark were wrangling happily over politics. He did not want to spend time showing Henby round the building, but took him for a quick glance at the finger-print department and the Records Office, duly impressed him, and then suggested that he might like to do a more comprehensive tour under the care of a sergeant.

"Take Lessing with you," Roger suggested. "He knows almost as much as I do."

"No one could!" Henby laughed. "I don't think I ought to stay this morning, but I'll come when you're not so busy. I ought to look in at the talk-shop, you know." He grinned. "After all, it's only just across the road."

"I shouldn't let your constituents hear you call the House the talk-shop."

"You ought to hear what they call it! Care to come with me, Lessing? I can guarantee you a lunch without a queue. Or with a very short queue."

"Thanks," said Mark. "I'd like to."

It was half an hour after the telephone call when Roger entered the A.C.'s office, but Chatworth was in a sunny mood.

"It's difficult for me to get into the Riddel social circle," Roger pointed out. "But Lessing already knows them, and might pick up one or two useful hints. What is more, he knows Henby, he's actually gone to the House with Henby now."

Chatworth said: "Are you thinking that Riddel might have been killed so that Henby and Mrs Riddel can get married?"

"We can't refuse to consider that possibility."

"No," admitted Chatworth. "I wouldn't want you to. And you can't stop Lessing from interfering, if he feels like doing so. But I've already told you of the extreme delicacy of this business. If Lessing were to do some silly thing and it was rumoured that we gave him our unofficial blessing——"

"We can't stop rumours, sir, and I don't think we ought to worry much about them. We want the murderers and we want to know why Riddel was killed. I'm prepared to adopt any method to find those things out."

Chatworth said abruptly:

"All right, use your own judgment. But warn Lessing we can't help him out if he gets into a mess of his own making. What else have you got on your mind?"

"I want to see Lord Plomley, interview Mrs Riddel formally, and go over all the ground," said Roger.

"Is there a report on Plomley's business interests?" he asked Sloan when he got back to his office.

"He's in everything as far as I can see," answered Sloan. "Boots and shoes take first place, but he's large interests in several chain stores. Rubber and textiles come next. After that he seems to have a finger in a dozen different pies. Chemicals, road transport, things like that. Of course, he's only on the financial side."

"Exactly what was the committee inquiring into?" asked Roger.

"Boots and shoes."

"So when he accepted the chairmanship of the committee, Riddel must have known that it would touch Plomley's affairs," reflected Roger. "Get the report out as soon as you can, won't you? Oh, another thing: who was Brayle holding a watching brief for this morning?"

"He handles all Plomley's business," said Sloan.

Roger thanked him, then he turned to the last report on his desk.

"At two-fifteen a.m., Mr Henby left the house by the fire-escape and walked across the waste ground between Ling Street and Cadargan Street, which is the next one to Ling Street. He then walked over Lambeth Bridge. I had difficulty in keeping him in sight, as he is a fast walker. I had arranged with D.O. Greenham to wait at the house, as instructions were not to leave the house unwatched. Mr Henby then walked through the back-streets to Queen Victoria Street, and eventually entered a house in Grosvenor Place, number 118g. He was there for fifty-five minutes. He left at one minute past four o'clock, and returned the way he had come."

"Well, well, well!" exclaimed Roger.

Eddie Day looked up. "Found something, Handsome?"

"Mysterious midnight marauding M.P.," burbled Roger. "Who lives at 118g, Grosvenor Place? Garner lives a few doors away, but——"

"118g is Plomley's place," Eddie told him. "I'm quite sure I'm right, because I happened to be passing Sloan on Monday morning, just after we started on this case, and Sloan said that Mrs Riddel had gone to her father's house, 118g, Grosvenor Place. Does it help?"

"Eddie, you're a marvel!" Roger meant it. "I'd give a fortune to have a memory like yours. Did Henby go to see his Cynthia at that bewitching hour or did he go to see Plomley? If Lessing rings up, tell him I'll see him about half-past four, will you?" He got up.

"What, here?"

"No, at Pansy's Café," said Roger. "Tell him I'll buy him some tea."

He was hardly outside the door, however, before it opened and Eddie Day put his nose into the passage and told him that Lessing was on the line. "And," declared Eddie, "he doesn't half sound pleased with himself. He wants taking down a peg or two. If I was you . . ."

Chapter Eleven

MARK'S LITTLE PIECE

"WELL," greeted Roger, "who killed Riddel, why did he or she kill Riddel? What was in that small parcel? How did the great man find the solution which has for so long been troubling the authorities, and would you like a knighthood in return for your services?"

"You're in a bright mood, aren't you?" queried Mark.

"The last words of Eddie Day were that you wanted taking down a peg or two, and I've done my best to oblige," said Roger, with a wink at Eddie. "He tells me that you sound disgustingly pleased with yourself."

"Not without cause," declared Mark. "I want to see you as soon as you can manage it."

"Won't the telephone do?"

"No. I'm in a call-box, and—well, I can't get my little piece off my chest over the telephone. Where and when?"

"I suppose I'd better see you right away," said Roger. "Pansy's in twenty minutes or so."

Roger walked to Pansy's Café, a tea-shop in Cannon Row, only a few minutes' from his office. Many years before it had been opened by a woman with so-called artistic ideas. The walls, furniture and crockery had been decorated with violet and yellow pansies, and on the facia board there was still the one word: Pansy's. Now, however, it was owned by Mario, a plump Italian who ran it with his wife; he kept on the right side of the Yard and Cannon Row, and had helped West on more than one occasion. It was a favourite haunt of the police, especially as Mario had an arrangement with a public-house nearby to obtain drinks.

At half-past three the place was almost empty, but Mark was sitting in one corner near the window, talking to Mario.

"And that is what I think," declared Mario. "Always it is the same, Inspector West do this, Inspector West do that, it is a great shame to spoil his holiday. Yes, I do think so."

"But does he?" asked Mark. "Hallo, Roger!"

Mario spun round. He wore a black coat and a white apron, and his thin black hair was oiled and brushed

carefully so that it crimped a little at the sides and forehead. He beamed a welcome. He sympathized. He
inquired after Janet and the bambinos. He promised the
best tea in London for them, and strutted off to prepare
this for them.

Roger sat down. Mark's smile was almost as broad as
Mario's.

"Happy?" asked Roger.

"I think you will be," Mark said. "Mario has promised
to keep other customers away for a time, so we can talk
freely. I've just left Henby."

Roger did not speak.

"He was as friendly as he could be," declared Mark.
"If he weren't such a character, he would have been
nauseating, he was so anxious to please me. The House of
Commons now has no secrets from me. I met two Cabinet
Ministers and three Parliamentary Private Secretaries."

"What did you do?"

"Behaved very properly, and gave him some 'inside information' on your general conviction that having caught
Tandy you would have the whole case sorted out within
a few days. I kept running off at a tangent, but he always
came back to the same subject. He actually mentioned
Plomley, and said what a coincidence it was that Riddel
should be on the committee which was investigating the
Plomley Trust, among other things. How does it sound?"

"Interesting."

"You ungrateful swab. I tell you that Henby showed a
most unhealthy interest in the case. He's like a cat on
hot bricks. Finished up by telling me that he was naturally
extremely interested, and that while he understood that
you, personally, could not keep him informed, he would
very much appreciate it if I did as much as I could to
keep him up to date with things. Oh, and he laid special
emphasis on the report he gave you about Riddel's
recent eccentricity and what-not."

"Good Lord!" exclaimed Roger. "I haven't read it yet."

"That would hurt his vanity. Where is it?"

"In my pocket. Did he tell you where he went between three and five o'clock this morning?"

Mark said: "Did he go out?"

"Yes, to Plomley's place."

"Did he, by George! He remarked that Cynthia Riddel is staying with her father, and the more I think about the possibility of Cynthia and Henby being behind it, the more I'm inclined to think they might be," Mark declared. "Don't you want to know what they talked about last night?"

"Yes," said Roger. "Henby once reminded me that a Member of Parliament is not above the law. You're going to be more useful than you realized."

"I don't like this under-cover business," Mark said. "If Chatworth would be reasonable——"

"He is being reasonable. I'm to use my discretion, and if you get yourself into any kind of trouble, you can't expect us to get you out of it. There was also the usual blah about the absolute need for discretion in this particular case. Mark, there isn't any real doubt that Chatworth is afraid that when we've finished we're going to uncover some ugly scandals. There's a lot of boiling water in this particular cauldron, and when the lid comes off we're going to see some nasty scum. What do you think is the most important thing to find out now?"

"You might explain——" Mark began, only to break off. "Here's Mario."

Mario came towards them, carrying a tray covered with a table-napkin. He placed the tray on the table, beamed, whipped off the napkin, and stood back, expectantly. There, in two china dishes, were strawberries, glistening and tempting, piled up high. On a second dish was a heap of clotted cream. Beside these the wafer-thin bread and butter and pastries seemed unimportant.

Roger said: "Marvellous!" His eyes glistened like a small boy.

"Well," said Mark, at last, "this ought to put you in a good humour. You always were a glutton for cream."

"For my health's sake," claimed Roger. "The most important and probably the most difficult part of the job now is finding a connection between Tandy and Company and one of our leading suspects. In short, Cynthia, Henby, Plomley and, possibly, Garner."

"I haven't given much thought to Garner," admitted Mark.

"Perhaps we haven't given enough," said Roger.

"Well, what do you want me to do?"

"Chiefly keep an eye on Cynthia," answered Roger. "We're watching her, but it isn't always easy, and you won't look so out of place at Scott's or the Savoy! You asked for the society angle. You've got it."

"Thanks. What are you going to do next?"

"What I would have been doing now if you hadn't telephoned," said Roger. "I'm going to see Plomley."

Plomley's house was a hundred yards away from Colonel Garner's. A manservant opened the door, and took Roger's card and asked him to wait. Two Van Goghs, perfect in his particular style, were the only pictures in the hall. Roger studied them, but he was alert for any sound. A door opened, but he did not glance round, and pretended to be surprised when Cynthia Riddel said:

"Good afternoon, Inspector."

Roger turned and beamed. "Hallo, Mrs Riddel!"

"Have you come to see me?"

"No," said Roger, "although I would like a few words with you while I'm here, if you can spare the time."

"Of course. Have you come to see my father?"

"Yes."

"I hope you won't have to worry him too much, Inspector."

"I won't ask him more than is absolutely necessary," Roger assured her.

"He has not been well for some months," she explained, "and the shock of my husband's death and the strain of what has followed is proving too much for him. I must not try to influence you, of course."

She smiled and turned away, walking with that peculiarly noticeable grace and distinction.

The manservant came down the stairs.

"His lordship will see you in a few minutes, sir, if you will please wait in the morning-room."

"Thanks," said Roger, and followed him into a small, pleasantly furnished room.

Soon Plomley came in, slowly, and the first thing that struck Roger was his pallor. He looked seriously ill. He was tall and well-built, and Roger recollected seeing him on ceremonial occasions, when he had been in radiant health, an impressive-looking man. There was nothing impressive-looking about him now. He was thin to the point of emaciation, and his eyes were dull.

One thing was certain: this had not all come about since Riddel's death.

"Good afternoon, Inspector." His low-pitched voice was firm enough. "Please sit down." He followed suit, and stretched his legs out in front of him. "I do not need telling about what business you have come, Inspector. I am, of course, at your service."

"Thank you, my lord," said Roger. "I hope that I shall not have to trouble you a great deal."

He asked several questions, none of them of great importance, chiefly about Riddel's movements and general state of health before the murder. Plomley answered easily yet all the time there was an undercurrent of nervousness in his manner. It showed in his eyes, in his rather tense expression when one question had been answered and he waited for another. The man seemed to be expecting something unpleasant, perhaps a question which he could not answer. He was on his guard, and he carefully considered every word before uttering it.

"I know you will understand that I speak in absolute confidence, sir, but I wonder if you can tell me whether Mr Riddel was friendly with the other members of the committee."

"Oh, I think so," said Plomley.

"Was he more friendly with any one of them than the others?"

"You must remember that I did not know my son-in-law particularly well," Plomley reminded him.

"Of course not," said Roger. "Was he on good terms with Mr Henby, do you know?"

"I know nothing to the contrary. They had known each other for some years," went on Plomley. "I really cannot help you very much in that direction, Inspector."

"Did Mr Riddel ever speak to you about a small brown paper packet, about the size of a flat tin of fifty cigarettes?"

There was a slight pause; an almost imperceptible change in Plomley's expression. "So that's it!" thought Roger. He waited, smiling expectantly, until Plomley said:
"No, Inspector."

"You didn't see such a thing in his possession?"

"Isn't that a somewhat unnecessary question?" demanded Plomley.

"I assure you I don't ask unnecessary questions," said Roger, and for the first time his voice grew sharp. The glint in Plomley's eyes encouraged him. Plomley was less composed now. "I have reason to believe that the packet is of great importance, Lord Plomley, and——"

"Don't lie to me sir!" Plomley rose to his feet and stood glaring down; like his daughter he had become a changed man. "I will not have such insolence! I have told you already that I know nothing about such a packet. Are you calling me a liar?"

Roger stood up. "I am sorry that you consider it necessary to be so offensive, my lord."

"Offensive! You are insolent! I insist you leave this house at once." Plomley's cheeks had flushed, he was clenching his hands, almost violently. "Do you hear me?"

"Clearly," said Roger. "You understand, of course, that in the interests of justice that packet must be found and its contents examined and——"

"Justice! What justice do you imagine——" Plomley choked, and Roger felt alarmed, for the man was well-nigh hysterical. But Plomley regained something of his composure, told Roger he did not wish to continue the discussion, and bade him good-day.

Roger paused with his hand on the handle of the door. "Mrs Riddel is going to see me for a few minutes and——"

"I shall not allow my daughter to be harassed any further! Already she has received a crushing blow. One would expect that men with ordinary common decency would know better than to distress her."

"Her husband was murdered," Roger reminded him.

Plomley actually raised his hand to strike him as the door opened. Cynthia came in. She took in the situation swiftly and stepped between them. She took her father's upraised arm with an almost caressing movement, slipped her other arm round his waist, and said:

"Come upstairs, Plum."

"Not while that man is in my house!" Plomley's voice was hoarse and quavering.

Cynthia looked at Roger.

"All right," Roger said, and went out; he walked slowly along the passage without looking back, and waited for the manservant to open the front door and show him out. He was so intent upon catching anything that either

Plomley or his daughter said that he did not hear the knock on the front door.

The door opened and Colonel Garner came in.

"Good afternoon, Sale. Is his lordship——"

Garner caught sight of Roger, and stopped. He looked rather like a scared rabbit, about to turn tail and bolt. Then he forced a smile and held out his hand in an excessive gesture of friendliness.

At the foot of the stairs, Plomley stood quivering and calling: "I won't see Garner. I'll see no one, no one, do you understand? No one!"

Cynthia tightened her grip on him, and led him upstairs.

Chapter Twelve

INTERVENTION OF A FAIR-HAIRED MAN

"I THINK we'd better go," Roger said.

Garner was staring at the couple on the stairs. He did not seem to hear Roger, who touched his arm.

"Oh, yes, yes," he said. "Has he had another seizure, Sale?"

"I am afraid so, sir," said the manservant.

"Pity," said Garner. He looked at Roger, his gaze suddenly frosty. "Is it your doing, West?"

"I don't think he can blame anyone but himself."

"I must say that I consider it most reprehensible to come at such a time."

"Oh, don't be a fool." Roger was too exasperated to be diplomatic.

He had not reached the pavement before he regretted his outburst. He glanced over his shoulder and saw Garner standing at the top of the steps, staring at him. From the man's expression, he knew that he had made a serious mistake, and one likely to bring repercussions. But what mattered now was the fact that he had antagonized Plomley.

He went towards Victoria, Garner towards Hyde Park. On the other side of the road was a C.I.D. man watching the Plomley residence. Roger crossed the road, seeing the man raise his hand, as if to indicate that he wanted to speak to him.

"Are you finding it dull?" asked Roger.

"It's all in the day's work, sir. There is one thing I thought you would like to know at once. Someone else has been watching Lord Plomley's residence and Colonel Garner's. He's not here now, sir. He saw you enter Lord Plomley's, and then went along to Colonel Garner's. He was admitted without any questions, and left a short while afterwards. A very few minutes after that Colonel Garner came out and went into Lord Plomley's."

"Well done," said Roger. "Did you get a good look at the man?"

"Oh, yes, sir. Well-dressed, fair, rather medium-sized, about five foot eight, I'd say. Grey eyes, fresh complexion—not florid, sir, just fresh. A man of about thirty, I would say, and he speaks with a cultured voice, sir."

"You've done well," Roger said.

"Thank you, sir. I happened to hear him speak to someone who passed just now. A woman, sir. She stopped only for a moment, but I think she came specially to see him. She passed on a message, very simply she said, 'Eight o'clock.' He said: 'That's fine, Susie'—I'm sure about the Susie, sir—and she walked on. A pretty little piece, sir, with a page-boy bob, not very noticeable but smart. I don't think the man has done much of this work before, sir, I'm sure he doesn't know who I am."

"Telephone the Yard, tell them that I said you were to be relieved at once, go to the Yard and get that description circulated to all London police stations. Tell Inspector Sloan first. If we can pick that man up, we might find something useful."

"Right, sir."

"One other thing," went on Roger. "Ask Inspector Sloan to try to get in touch with Mr Mark Lessing and pass the description on to him."

Roger went on his way, passing a kiosk which the C.I.D. man used and entered another near Victoria Station. He rang Plomley's house, and was answered by the manservant with whom he had already spoken. He asked for Cynthia, and was told that she was engaged.

"Tell her this is important," Roger said.

"Is that Mr Henby?" asked the manservant.

"Never mind—tell her," said Roger.

He was kept waiting for several minutes before Cynthia came on the line. She sounded as if she had been hurrying and her first words were:

"George, I must see you——"

Roger interrupted: "I think there is some mistake, Mrs Riddel. This is Inspector West."

She did not say another word, and was obviously pulling herself together, and her breathing, quick at first, became normal. The pause lasted for so long that Roger began to wonder whether she had rung off. Then she said in an aloof voice:

"You will want to see me, I suppose?"

"Please," said Roger. "Shall I call at your house?"

"I think it will be wiser if I come to see you. Will you be at your office in an hour's time?"

"Yes."

"I will see you there," she promised.

Roger was smiling very tensely: That "George, I must see you," had given a great deal away.

He drove along Grosvenor Place, and parked the car within sight of 118g. The C.I.D. man had been relieved and had hurried off. Roger watched Plomley's residence, hoping that Henby would arrive. He did not, but ten minutes after their telephone conversation, Cynthia came

out and beckoned a taxi. Roger started the engine and let
in the clutch. He followed her taxi, which went towards
Hyde Park and turned into the gateway. There Roger was
unlucky, for the lights were against him. He waited
impatiently, cursing his luck, when a small Morris passed
him, ignored the lights and swept across the road. A
policeman called out and a bus swerved dangerously. The
Morris went on. Roger wasted no more time, as the cross-
wise traffic was at a standstill, but followed the Morris,
which drove too fast through the park. As they approached
Marble Arch, Roger saw it drawing near Cynthia's taxi,
a green one easily recognizable. After that, the driver of
the little Morris was content to follow leisurely.

Roger tried to catch a glimpse of him, but did not
succeed until it turned down by Selfridges. Then he saw
that the man was fair-haired.

Cynthia got out of her taxi in Wigmore Street. The
Morris drove past. Roger pulled up some distance away,
the Morris stopped farther ahead. Cynthia said something
over her shoulder to the driver, and hurried inside the
house. Roger picked up an old newspaper, and pretended
to read. The fair-haired man got out of the Morris, and
there was no doubt that it was the man who had already
been reported. He stood outside the house, studying the
brass plates, and then suddenly he looked round, started
and hurried away.

A man was passing Roger's car.

Roger buried his head in the newspaper, recognizing
Henby. Henby might have recognized him had he not
been watching the fair-haired man. He looked furiously
angry, and once almost broke into a run. Then he
steadied down. He went into the same house as Cynthia,
after having had a good stare at the fair-haired man, who
seemed uncertain what to do next.

Then a low-lying sports car passed Roger's, and the
driver sounded a deep, braying note on his horn. Startled,

Roger looked round, and saw Mark Lessing at the wheel of a Lagonda. Mark did not wave, or show any other sign of recognition, but he pulled into the kerb just behind the Morris. The driver of the Morris was getting into his car again.

"Gathering of the clans," murmured Roger. "I suppose Mark followed Henby." He looked round, and caught sight of a police-constable some distance along the street. Roger got out of the car and beckoned him, and the man hurried up.

"Did you want me, sir?"

"Yes," said Roger. "I want you to deliver a message."

Mark did not even look round as the policeman passed, but a moment later he raised his right-hand as if to acknowledge the message. Roger decided that he would be better away from Wigmore Street, and drove back the way he had come, through the parks to Whitehall. He was in his office and had about twenty minutes to spare before Cynthia Riddel was due to see him. He telephoned Sloan, told him what had developed and that he was to watch the fair-haired man; it could not be left entirely to Mark.

"If you're quick, you might catch him in Wigmore Street," Roger said. "Don't interfere with Mark Lessing."

"Okay!" said Sloan. "I'd better get going."

Exactly an hour after Roger had telephoned Cynthia Riddel, the telephone rang, and he expected to be told that she was waiting for him downstairs. Instead, it was a disappointed Sloan. Both the cars and the taxi had left Wigmore Street before he had arrived.

"Oh, well," said Roger. "We'll have to wait until we hear from Mark. He'll send word as soon as something turns up." He replaced the receiver and waited for the call announcing Mrs Riddel. He waited for an hour, but there was no word from her.

Nor was there any message from Mark.

In high spirits, Mark Lessing left Pansy's Café and walked across the road towards his car. He did not know exactly where to start, and sat at the wheel of the Lagonda, turning over the situation in his mind. Roger, he thought, had definitely plumped for Henby as a priority suspect. The right thing to do was to get in touch with as many of Henby's friends as he could, especially those who also knew Cynthia Riddel. He was about to drive off when an acquaintance recognized him. Mark could not get away from him for over ten minutes, and when at last he did start off, he saw Henby hurrying out of the courtyard of the Houses of Parliament. Something in the M.P.'s manner attracted Mark's attention; he put on the handbrake and watched as Henby stopped a passing taxi. Then he followed the taxi.

Henby went straight to Wigmore Street and, a few minutes afterwards, Mark received the message, which Roger had passed on through the policeman, to tail Cynthia.

It was not long before Cynthia came out, on her own, and drove off in the waiting taxi.

The man in the Morris followed her.

"Now we're really starting," murmured Mark.

It was a dull enough drive for a quarter of an hour, but once or twice Mark caught sight of Riddel's widow glancing through the back window of the cab. Then the taxi turned right. Mark got the impression that it was making a detour in the hopes of shaking off the pursuing Morris. The driver of the Morris jammed on his brakes and turned after it, without giving any signal. Mark followed suit, hearing the squealing of brakes behind him. The taxi was bowling along at a good pace, but the Morris kept up. Several quick, bewildering turns did not shake the man off, and, near Piccadilly, the cab pulled up quickly.

Cynthia Riddel got out.

She glanced once at the fair-haired driver of the Morris,

and then turned to join the crowd, but the Morris driver left his car and went after her. Mark pulled up, and followed leisurely; he thought it unlikely that Cynthia would get away. At last, the man caught up with Cynthia. He touched her arm, and said something which Mark had no chance of hearing.

She stopped.

The fair-haired man went on talking, almost pleading. Cynthia looked at the man coldly, and did not speak, but with obvious reluctance turned and followed him to his car.

Mark started off before the Morris. He allowed the little car to overtake him, then followed at what seemed a discreet distance. The familiar road to Victoria made him wonder whether they were driving to Plomley's home, but the car turned left along Buckingham Palace Gate, drove through Sloane Square, Chelsea and Fulham, and turned left to go over Putney Bridge.

"They must have seen me by now," Mark thought, feeling uneasy for the first time.

They pulled up at a corner of a short road leading to the river, left the Morris there, and hurried along it. There were several large houses, standing in their own grounds and overlooking the river. The fair-haired man kept a hand on Cynthia's arm and they turned into the drive of the second house.

Mark got out of the Lagonda, feeling very conspicuous.

A man came out of the gateway of the house nearest the river and walked briskly towards him. Mark was making certain that he could not be seen from the house into which Cynthia had gone, and gave him little attention. He was taken completely by surprise when the man passed him, stopped, swung on his heel and struck at him with a weapon he could not see. It caught Mark a glancing blow on the head, making him lose his balance. The man jumped forward and hooked his legs from under him.

Mark was helpless as the other bent over him and smashed his weapon on the top of his head and he just caught a glimpse of a familiar-looking cosh as the blow fell.

The man shoved the cosh into his pocket and dragged Mark by the heels into the nearest drive-way. Then he stood still, recovering his breath, before dragging Mark farther into the bushes of a nearby garden. He felt his pulse, seemed satisfied, took off his tie and bound his wrists behind him. Next, he stuffed a handkerchief into Mark's mouth. Then he picked up a couple of armfuls of dead leaves and threw them over the inert body.

He strolled to the gate and looked up and down, then went into the house where Cynthia and the fair-haired man were waiting.

By seven o'clock, Roger was really alarmed.

A call had already gone out for Mark and Cynthia Riddel, but there were no reports in. Most of the men had left the Yard, and only occasional footsteps echoed up and down the stone corridors. Roger looked alternately at his watch and out of the window. The telephone in the next office rang, and made him start. Angry with himself, he was about to leave his office when his own telephone rang.

He snatched it up. "Hallo? West speaking."

"Henby here," said Henby, abruptly. "Do you know where Mrs Riddel is?"

"I've no idea," said Roger. "Why?"

"She was to have met me at six o'clock," said Henby. "She hasn't turned up."

"Women have been known to be late for appointments," Roger reminded him.

"Don't be a fool," said Henby. "This was important. I'm afraid something might have happened to her. You're sure you haven't seen her lately?"

Roger said: "The last time I saw her was in Wigmore Street."

Henby snapped: "Do you mean she didn't come to see you?"

"No. You're very well informed, aren't you?"

"Never mind that," snapped Henby. "West, you must find her. Take my word for it, she is in considerable danger. I can't explain, but——"

"We've already given general instructions for a watch to be kept for her," Roger told him. "There's nothing more we can do about that. Isn't it time you stopped playing the fool with the police?"

Henby said: "What I do is my business."

"What Mrs Riddel does is my business."

"Be damned to you," growled Henby. "Get on with your job and find her. After that I might be able to give you some help."

"You can start now," said Roger. "Henby, if you ring off, I'll have you detained as a material witness. I'm not fooling."

After a pause, Henby said: "So you're getting tough."

"I can be tough," Roger growled. "Who is the fair-haired man you saw in Wigmore Street? There's a good reason to think that he might know where Mrs Riddel is."

"I know he's often at a club behind Shaftesbury Avenue—the Swing Club, you probably know it."

"He's an intellectual, is he?" said Roger.

"He's a member there," Henby repeated. "I don't know where else you'll find him."

"All right, thanks," said Roger. "Don't play the fool, Henby."

He rang off, without giving Henby a chance to answer, picked up the other telephone and asked for Sloan. "Bill," he said, "we're going to the Swing Club in Soho, and we'd better be there in force. The fair-haired man is an habitué, and the eight o'clock meeting he arranged this afternoon might be held there. I think you'd better arrange for half a dozen men to watch the club from now on, and you and I will go along about a quarter to eight. We'll wait about to see if our man goes in. Oh, who was the officer on duty in Grosvenor Place this afternoon?"

"Do you mean Winneger?" asked Sloan. "Oldish, dark——"

"Yes, Winneger's the man. He'd better be with you and me, as he saw the girl who gave Fair-hair the message. All right?"

"Yes. Er—Roger?"

"Yes?"

"If you're expecting trouble, oughtn't we to be prepared this time?"

"Meaning guns," said Roger. "I think you're right."

Roger telephoned Abbott, who always seemed to be on duty, arranged for three guns and twelve rounds of ammunition each, then had some difficulty in getting in touch with the Inspector whose duty it was to keep the clubs in the West End under surveillance. The Swing Club, he was assured, had an unblemished reputation. He could never understand why it had been given such a name. It was primarily a debating society, although they had a licence for music and dancing. He had heard nothing at all against any of the members. The secretary was a man named Johns, Walter Johns, a long-haired intellectual.

Sloan came in, carrying two automatics in one hand and one in the other.

"A present from Abbott," he said.

"That man doesn't lose time," admitted Roger. "Is everything set?"

"The first lot of men are there by now," Sloan assured him, as they went out of the office. "Are you seriously expecting trouble, Roger?"

"Yes," said Roger.

They did not speak again until they were driving through the dusk towards Soho.

Chapter Thirteen

THE SWING CLUB

THE club was in a corner building, along a narrow turning which led off from Shaftesbury Avenue. It was already dusk when Roger, Sloan and Winneger arrived. They parked in a side turning, and spoke to the sergeant in charge of the first party.

"A few have gone in," he said, "but there isn't much sign of life yet. I'm told it doesn't usually warm up till nine o'clock. Our man hasn't arrived, sir, that's certain."

Roger stood with Sloan and Winneger, behind the cover of a wall only six feet high, and watched the entrance to the club. In ten minutes, three people entered it. All were young and two were of the artist type; the third was a business-like looking man. There was a gap of five minutes, and a nearby clock was striking eight when a taxi pulled up opposite the club. Roger stepped forward to see the passenger more clearly. Winneger was with him.

"That's her, sir."

"Well, she was on time," said Roger. "Well done, Winneger!"

"Fair-hair ought to be along soon," said Sloan.

"He'll come. I—ah, here's the Morris!"

The little car swung off the road on to the asphalt pavement of a bombed-out building. The fair-haired man, only just visible, got out, slammed and locked the door, then went into the club. He had not switched on the lights of the car. He did not look round, and seemed unaware of being followed.

"When do we move in?" asked Sloan.

"We'll close in now," said Roger.

He gave a prearranged signal to the sergeant-in-charge. The watching policemen left their hiding places and advanced. Their instructions were to prevent anyone from coming out, and to question everyone who wanted to go in. Roger, Sloan and Winneger, with automatics in their pockets, went into the tiny entrance hall. There was only a dim light, which showed a door marked "Cloaks" and a flight of stairs covered with cheap drugget. Their footsteps were loud as they went up the stairs. The strains of music from a radio filtered down from one of the rooms.

Two doors, one open and one closed, faced them. Beyond the open one was a counter, at which a skinny girl sat filing her nails. She looked up when Roger entered and her eyes widened.

"You a member?" she asked.

"No," said Roger.

"I didn't think you was," she said. "Visitors are only allowed with a member. Sorry, that's the rule. No, it isn't any use showing me your card . . . Strewth!"

Roger said: "Be a good girl and keep your head. We're here on business, and——"

"You can't raid this place," she objected. "Don't be silly! Why, there's not even a game of dominoes here! You're wasting your time."

"We want to interview one or two of the members," Roger said. "Tell me where the main rooms are, will you?"

"That's easy. Through the other door, along the passage. Dining-room on your right, bar straight in front of you, lounge on your left. That's the club."

"What about the offices?"

"Oh, they're upstairs," she said. "No one's up there now."

"Sure?"

"Well, I haven't seen anyone go up."

Roger turned to Winneger. "Stay here, sergeant. No one is to talk with this young lady, and no one is to go down the stairs. We'll have a look round upstairs, Bill." He led the way up another flight of druggeted stairs to a landing much smaller than that on the first floor. There were two doors, one marked *General*, the other marked *Private*. There was no light beneath either door, but there was a single pale lamp above their heads.

"It looks as if she's right," said Sloan. He tried one of the handles. "Locked," he added, superfluously.

"This one isn't," said Roger.

The second door opened into a small room, and they could only just see the walls in the poor light. He groped for the light switch. Two lamps came on, covered with white glass shades, and they narrowed their eyes against the brilliance. Soon, they were able to take in the contents of the room. It was the one marked *Private*. There was a roll-top desk in one corner and a typist's desk at another. The shelves were filled with books, and a cursory examination showed them to be mostly on political and economic theory. A few copies of Hansard were among them, and there were sheafs of untidy papers.

"Dull and frowsty," declared Sloan.

"Yes," said Roger. "It's odd, you know. Only two rooms, as small as this, and there are several rooms on the floor below. Did you notice whether there was a sloping roof?"

"No."

"I think we'll try and get next door," said Roger.

"Oughtn't we to be getting downstairs?" Sloan objected.

"In a moment," promised Roger. He took a stout penknife from his pocket, went into the passage and tried the other door. It was useless to try to open it with the knife, and for the first time he examined the lock. "That's odd," he said. "A new special safety lock for the general office, and an old-fashioned back-door lock for the private one." He examined the lock more closely. "We'll need crowbars to open that," he declared, "and I wouldn't be surprised to find it's steel."

"What!"

Roger tapped it. It gave off a faintly hollow note, with a slight ringing sound, and was cold to the touch. "Steel painted over to look like grained wood," he said. "Probably fire-proof." He laughed, without amusement. "There's more in the Swing Club even than we bargained for, and——"

Sloan cried: "Look out, Roger!"

At the same moment he thrust out his hand and pushed Roger sideways. Roger did not see what happened, but he heard a heavy thud and then saw a man lurching forward from the momentum of a heavy blow. The man's back was towards the open door of the private office. He was a little fellow, and his face showed surprise and alarm. Sloan jumped forward and gripped his arm.

"That's enough," he said.

The little man recovered enough to kick Sloan on the shins and force him to release his grip. Another blow, this time at Roger, missed by inches. Roger shot out his fist and caught the man on the side of the jaw. It hurt his hand, and it certainly hurt the man, who backed away, dazed.

"That's more than enough," said Roger.

In their assailant's right hand was a leather-covered cosh. He raised it, but Roger wrested it from him and examined it closely. It was familiar enough; the inside was filled with lead shot, and a blow from it would knock a man out without showing much bruising or scratching.

"So you're quite an old hand," murmured Roger. "Weren't you a bit rash?" He pushed the man into the private office, following him into the room; the room was exactly as it had been when he had looked at it a few minutes before.

"Where did you come from?" he demanded.

"You can go fry your face."

"That's enough!" Roger spoke sharply. "Run through

his pockets, Bill." He held the man so that he could not resist, and Sloan emptied his pockets. Sloan brought out a small automatic and a bunch of keys. "They'll be a help," he added. "I think one of these will fit the room next door, but——" He turned and glared at the little man.

"Where did you come from?"

There was still no answer.

"Perhaps the desk moves," suggested Sloan.

"There are times when I'd like to use violence," declared Roger. "He could tell us in a moment." He went to the desk and examined it; there did not appear to be anything amiss. He bent down and looked at the knee-hole in the front. This was large enough for a small man to hide in, and they had not searched the room closely. "I don't think there's any mystery about that. Let's go next door and try the key."

A voice said: "Don't move!"

It came from above their heads, and they looked up involuntarily. They could see no one, but they could see the muzzle of a gun pointing at them from a small hole near the ceiling.

"Don't move." The voice came again. "Let him go."

Roger said: "Now don't play the fool. The place is full of police, and——"

"It won't be full of you if you don't let him go!"

Roger dropped his hand to his pocket.

"All right, Bill," he said, as if disgusted. "We can't argue with a gun." He gripped his own gun, inside his pocket, and pointed it upwards. It was difficult to judge the direction. Sloan let the prisoner go, and the man shrugged his coat into position and moved to pick up the bunch of keys.

Roger fired.

The bullet struck the wood near the hole, and the gun disappeared. Sloan grabbed the prisoner again, and

although the little man tried to get away, Sloan treated
him rough and swung him against the desk. The keys fell
from his fingers. Sloan picked them up as a shot was fired
through the wall. It splintered the partition as if it were
paper, and they heard the thud as the bullet struck the far
side of the room.

Roger dodged out of the doorway, on Sloan's heels.
The little man was still slumped down against the desk,
where Sloan had left him. There was a heavy thump from
the other room, and someone spoke in a low-pitched,
rumbling voice.

"There's only one way."

"Over the roof?" This voice was pitched on a higher
key.

"Shut up, you fool!"

"But what about her?"

"Never mind her," said the man with the rumbling
voice. "Watch that door. They can't get in while you're
covering it."

Roger jerked his thumb towards the stairs, and Sloan
hurried down to warn the men below. Roger stood back,
taking stock of the landing and the ceiling. There was no
way that he could see of getting to the roof. He heard one
of the policemen hurrying up the stairs, beckoned him and
whispered:

"Telephone for a fire-escape, and hurry about it."

"Right, sir."

"Then get more men and see that no one can get out,"
Roger went on. He watched the man run off, and then for
the first time he tried the keys in the lock of the door. The
third key fitted. He turned the lock and, standing a little
to one side, pushed the door open an inch. Immediately
there was a shot, the sound much louder than the first had
been. A bullet hit the banisters.

Roger said: "That's seven years for you, my lad."

The gunman did not answer.

"Unless you change your mind, drop the gun and open the door wide," continued Roger. "I might be able to help you if you'll do that."

The man said nothing.

"You might remind your friends that if anything happens to the woman in there, all of you will go down for life," went on Roger. He was waiting for one of the other men to come up, but before anyone appeared there was a scuffle downstairs, and a man shouted:

"What the devil do you mean? Keep your hands off me!"

"Sorry, sir. I've got my orders." That was Winneger.

"Damn your orders! I can come and go as I please."

"Now be reasonable, sir, please," Winneger protested.

He came into sight on the first floor landing, accompanied by a man with a shock of black hair, a pale face and a red tie. Roger thought his shirt was purple.

"Be reasonable!" he protested, in a squeaking voice. "You have the nerve to try to stop me leaving my own club, and ask me to be reasonable. Why, I——"

"Put the handcuffs on him if he's troublesome," Roger called down.

The man looked up, startled, and snatched his hands away. Abruptly he turned and disappeared into a room. There was a chorus of voices, someone laughed, another man swore. Three or four men appeared on the landing and Roger thought that Winneger began to look slightly apprehensive.

Roger called down: "If you people know what's good for you, you'll go back and wait until we authorize you to leave. This is a police raid."

"Good lord!" That was a woman's voice. "He means it!"

"I certainly do," said Roger, "and——"

Next moment, he bitterly blamed himself for his carelessness. For a few moments he had taken his eyes off the door. He heard the shot and felt the stinging pain in his left arm at the same time. It was sharp enough to make him stagger against the wall. The door slammed before he could hope to get his gun out.

"Are you all right, sir?" called Winneger.

"Yes," replied Roger. He fired from his pocket as he kicked the door open and the man who had wounded him was so startled that he did not even fire his gun. The bullet caught him in the chest and drove him backwards. There was no one in sight behind him, and he seemed to be in some sort of narrow passage.

Then a woman gasped: "No. No!"

He could not tell whether it was Cynthia Riddel or someone else; all he recognized was the desperate fear in that second "No!" A man swore, roughly, and there was a scuffling sound. A gasp followed, then a thump.

Two men were running up the stairs towards Roger.

The desperate urgency in the woman's voice made him go on, against all reasonable precaution. He slipped into the passage, and saw that it ran all the way round an inner room, the door of which was standing open. He could not see inside. He heard the clanging of a fire-engine bell; it was so loud that he knew a window was open. He stepped towards the door, the gun in his hand, and caught a glimpse of Mrs Riddel, with her back close to the window and clutching the frame. She was trying to kick a man whose hands were on her shoulders, forcing her backwards. The expression on the woman's face was one of sheer horror.

The man was trying to push her into the street below.

C.I.D. men reached the passage.

The man at the window caught hold of the woman's legs and heaved, and she screamed and toppled backwards. Roger leapt forward, grabbing at her with his right hand, trying to sweep the man aside with his left. He had no strength in it, but the man had not expected him, and lost his balance. Roger caught the woman by one foot, but as he did so her body slipped over the window sill and his grasp on her ankle weakened, the shoe beginning to slip off. Her knees were bent, he could now see only her legs; she was hanging head-first over the street below, and unless he could strengthen his grip she would fall.

Chapter Fourteen

REST FOR ROGER

THE shoe nearly came off.

Roger was making a supreme effort and tried to raise his left arm in support. He could not; there was no strength in it, although he felt no pain. The shoe was slipping again. With difficulty, he edged his hand up and grasped the woman by the leg. His fingers slipped about her stocking, and he thought he had lost her. Then his grip tightened, but her weight pulled him up against the window frame, banging his wounded arm.

There were sounds behind him. A man was swearing wildly and there was a bumping, thumping noise. Some-one fell against Roger, and knocked the wind out of him. He hardly knew whether he still held the woman's leg or whether he had let go. Then someone spoke calmly.

"All right, Roger."

Sloan climbed on to the window ledge, but he could not give immediate help. "Hold on!" he called, and squatted down cautiously. "Use your other hand." He stretched down, trying to clutch Cynthia's clothes. Roger could see the perspiration on his face and the veins standing out on his forehead. "Other arm!" gasped Sloan. Helplessly, Roger shook his head. The thumping was still going on behind him.

"What——" a man said, and then gasped: "Strewth!" He jumped forward, and Roger recognized Winneger. "Half a mo'!"

"Take over from me," Roger managed to say, "I can't hold on."

"Okay, sir."

Winneger had hardly room to get to the window, which was blocked on one side by Roger and the other by Sloan, but he wedged himself in sideways, stood on tip-toe, and gripped the woman's leg below and above the knee. Sloan gripped her by her clothes.

"All safe, sir."

Roger let go, staggered, then leaned against the wall. He tried to stand upright, but nearly fell. Now there was pain in his left arm, between the shoulder and the elbow. It was agonizing, and he bit his lips. The dizziness grew easier, but he was still unsteady when another man hurried in. By then, Sloan and Winneger were carrying Mrs Riddel back into the room. Sloan had one arm about her waist, and Winneger had tucked her legs beneath his arm. The man who had tried to push her out was on the floor, still struggling, and a C.I.D. man was bending over him.

"Well, she can think herself lucky," said Sloan. "How you held on to her, I don't know, Roger. I—good lord, man, what's the matter with you?"

"Do I look like a wax-work too?" asked Roger. "I'll be all right. What's happened outside?" He was suddenly alarmed; where were the men who had been in the room? Presumably they had climbed out before Cynthia, but he had to know. "What's happening?" He tried to get up, but a wave of nausea made him drop down in his chair again.

"We'll soon see," declared Sloan.

Leaving Cynthia in Winneger's charge, Sloan went to the window, leaned well out and peered along the roof-tops. For a moment he said nothing; when he broke his silence there was a harsh note in his voice.

"The light's bad, but they're getting away," he said.

"Two of them are running over the roofs as if they're monkeys."

"Where are your men?" demanded Roger.

"Climbing up. I——"

Sloan broke off, hoisted himself up and climbed through the window. He called back reassuringly to Roger as he reached the roof and started the chase. Then came the loud clanging of a fire-engine bell. Almost at the same moment, the C.I.D. man returned with a woman of about thirty, a well-dressed, competent-looking woman. The C.I.D. man looked apologetic.

"This lady's a doctor, sir."

"Have a look at the other patient first, will you?" asked Roger. "Winneger, lend me a hand. And you." He looked up at the C.I.D. man and then started to get up. He could not have managed it without their help. He forgot Cynthia and the woman doctor, reached the window, and stared out. Sloan was climbing over the roofs as quickly as his quarry. Distant street lamps and electric signs now gave a fair light. Roger saw one of the other two fugitives disappear behind a chimney stack. The second was walking along the edge of a roof, balancing himself with his arms outstretched.

He was a fair-haired man.

Below, the fire-engine had pulled up and the escape was being swung into position.

A sergeant was directing operations. Several men were running along the narrow street which ran parallel with Shaftesbury Avenue, and in the distance there was the sound of another fire-engine bell.

Roger concentrated on Sloan.

With surprising agility, Sloan went over the roof-tops, and was gaining on the others. They did not seem to realize they were being pursued so closely. Two other C.I.D. men reached the roof from another window, and followed Sloan. By then a crowd had gathered in the streets below, and Roger glanced down and saw their upturned faces; they looked unreal.

The fire-engine was in the wrong place, now; the crew began to wind the escape down.

"Is there another victim," asked the woman doctor, patiently.

Roger looked round. "Yes, I've a bullet in my arm."

The woman doctor helped him off with his coat, the sleeve of which was wet with blood. His shirt sleeve had soaked up much of the blood, and prevented it from dripping, and the sight was enough to turn Roger's stomach.

"Here, you!" the woman called to Winneger, who turned, startled. "There's a cloak-room across the passage, with a first-aid cabinet." She was rolling up the sleeve, and the blood got all over her fingers; a spot touched the cuff of her white silk blouse. "You'll have a bill for damages," she said, dryly. "What kind of a party is this?"

"Bloody," said Roger.

She laughed. "I can see that. Apart from the excitement outside, there is a howling mob of angry club members in the next room. All these alarms and excursions have scared them, and they aren't very pleased with you at the moment. Can't they go?"

"No."

"Does that also apply to me?"

"You can have privileged treatment, and be the first to be questioned," Roger said. "No one can go out without telling us why they're here, what they've been doing and——"

"Just routine?" asked the woman doctor.

"Rather more than routine," said Roger. "Er—do you mind? Talking makes my head swim."

She nodded, and did not speak again. Winneger brought in the first-aid box, and another man brought a towel, some hot water and a sponge. The arm grew increasingly painful and he quite expected that the bullet had shattered the bone. Sitting with her eyes still closed, Cynthia Riddel seemed to be regaining some colour. The man whom Roger had shot and the man who had tried to push Cynthia out of the window were no longer in the room.

"The bullet went straight through," said the doctor, in her brisk, businesslike voice. "I'll have to get you to hospital. I haven't the equipment here to make a good job of it. I'll be on duty from midnight onwards," she said, "so come to the Westminster."

A cry from the crowd outside made her stop, and made Roger jump to his feet. It was a curious sound, half-roar, half-sigh, and someone screamed. As the sounds faded there was another, farther away, like the screech of a siren; another scream, nearer at hand, and then a sound from some way off, a heavy, thudding sound.

Winneger turned excitedly: "Someone's fallen off the roof."

"Is it Inspector Sloan?"

"I can't really be sure, sir."

It seemed an age before he was being driven to the Westminster Hospital, with the doctor by his side. Then, as they turned into Shaftesbury Avenue, Roger saw Superintendent Abbott at the wheel of a small car, coming towards them. Well, Abbott would take charge and he would be compelled to rely on reports again. Mark still missing, Sloan perhaps dead, the men detained at the club ready for interrogation, and he in hospital. He groaned aloud.

No one ever questioned Superintendent Abbott's efficiency. The trouble was that he lacked the human touch. He did not, for instance, think of sending a message to Roger to tell him that one of the fugitives over the roof had been killed by a fall, that the other escaped, that none of the other police had been hurt and that soon after the excitement was over, the Putney police telephoned to report that Mark Lessing had been found in the garden of a large empty house at Putney—next door to the house where Cynthia had been taken. A passer-by had heard him calling for help.

It was Chatworth, wearing a glistening mackintosh and goloshes as a protection against the rain, now falling heavily, who told him.

"So all you've got to worry about, Roger, is getting better," he finished. "What do they say about that arm? Are they looking after you all right?"

"There's no reason why I shouldn't be about in a couple of days," said Roger. "I was going to ask you to telephone Janet at once, sir, and make sure that she doesn't think I'm badly hurt," said Roger.

"I'll do that," Chatworth promised. "Now, about Lessing. He was knocked out but soon recovered. He has identified the man who attacked him—the same man, apparently, whom you and Sloan first found at the Swing Club. He has also told us where Mrs Riddel was taken before they brought her on here—it doesn't get us very far, I'm afraid. The house is owned by the man Tandy."

"Does Tandy own a big house in Putney?"

"He bought it some time ago and let it furnished so has been back there only a few months. There must be big profits in trick cycling!" He went on: "Now Roger, this is important. I wouldn't come to see you about it tonight otherwise. Mrs Riddel tells us that this fair-haired man questioned her only about the brown-paper packet. She declares that she does not know what was in it, but that he wanted some information about it. Now, we know that Tandy took that packet from you, don't we? Yet the fair-haired man wants it. The fair-haired man apparently has the freedom of Tandy's house, so that doesn't make sense."

"No," murmured Roger.

Chatworth asked abruptly: "Do you think Mrs Riddel was telling the truth?"

"Well, I believe that she would lie to us," declared Roger. "If it suited her and if she thought it wise, she wouldn't hesitate. I don't know about this particular packet, of course. She brought me a packet which was supposed to be the one in question, remember. What has she to say about that?"

"All she says is that the fair-haired man—he's got a name, why shouldn't we use it?—wanted information about a small brown-paper packet. She isn't herself yet, by any means. She had a great shock. Very nice piece of work on your part, and it won't be forgotten."

He picked up his hat.

"Just a moment!" exclaimed Roger. "There are several things, sir. First, what is the fair-haired man's name?"

"O'Dare. Irish extraction, English upbringing. Well-educated as far as I can make out. He was the one who escaped over the roofs."

"He persuaded Mrs Riddel to go with him, and I'm quite sure they are old acquaintances," said Roger.

"Well, she hasn't yet told us anything more about him," declared Chatworth. "Yes, I know, she's keeping something back. We could detain her, of course, but I'm reluctant to do so."

"I'd leave her free, and watch her," said Roger.

"I quite agree," said Chatworth.

"What else happened at the club?" Roger asked.

"Very little, Roger. No one among the members seems to know anything about the happenings in the office. The fortified room was a surprise to them all. There isn't anything the matter with the club as a club, I'm sure of that. It's the officials who have been up to some funny business. Johns, the secretary, was the man who fell off the roof and killed himself. The other men who were caught appear to be hangers-on. I don't know much about them, and they're being questioned now."

"Did Mrs Riddel say why she went to Wigmore Street?" Roger asked.

"She isn't being frank about seeing Henby there," said Chatworth, "but apparently she met him at the home of a friend who lives in the street."

Roger was glad when Chatworth left. He felt too tired to think clearly, and all he wanted to do was sleep.

It was still raining when he woke up.

Sometime later, the door opened and a nurse said: "Here he is."

Roger looked up, as Janet came hurrying into the room.

Chapter Fifteen

CONVALESCENCE

"OF course, I didn't believe Chatworth," said Janet, her sun-tanned face close to his. "I caught the first train I could. He didn't tell me until eight o'clock this morning, the marvel is that I hadn't read the papers by then. What are you going to do now? You can't stay in this pigsty for long."

Roger laughed. "Is pigsty the word?"

"You know what I mean," said Janet. "They're not going to make you work as soon as you can get up, are they? I think I'll go and see Chatworth."

"Don't do that," protested Roger, hastily. "I can manage him, you've had quite enough to say to him on this job!"

It was pleasant just to sit there, with Janet's fingers getting warmer in his hand. It was pleasant to close his eyes, and surprisingly easy, for a short while, not to think of the Riddel case. It would be good to return to Bognor. There was a balcony at the hotel, on which he could

sit and watch the sea and the passing crowds on the promenade. Very pleasant . . . Hallo, someone was talking,
talking. Who was it? Great Scott, he'd been to sleep. And
Janet was speaking sharply, although in a low-pitched
voice. He could always tell when Janet was angry. There
was a man talking to her . . .

He opened his eyes.

"But it is really important," George Henby was
saying.

"Nothing can be so important that you need wake
him up," declared Janet. "I'm surprised that the
nurse——"

"Hallo, there," murmured Roger.

Janet swung round, and Henby pushed past her.

"Roger, it's too bad!" Janet was flushed with annoyance,
and Roger thought that she had probably been arguing
with Henby for some time. "He's no right to come in here
like this."

"He's no right to do a lot of things that he does,"
Roger assured her, sitting up on his pillows. "He keeps
information from the police, which is excessively bad
policy for a Member of Parliament. The police get ideas."
He felt refreshed and able to cope.

"Do you two know each other? Darling, this is George
Henby, Henby, my wife."

"Oh, lord!" exclaimed Henby. "Now I have put my
foot in it. I thought I was talking to a particularly attractive—eh—nurse who was off duty!" But he gave Janet
his most engaging smile, and in spite of her annoyance,
her expression grew less angry. "I wouldn't have come
had I not thought it really important, West."

"The police force works without me," Roger reminded
him.

"You get a grasp of things quicker than most, and you
know this situation inside out. I would have gone to see
Lessing, but I can't find him. I think Chatworth has

secreted him away, in case someone else tries to break his neck."

Henby sat down on the bedside chair.

"It's about this fair-haired fellow, O'Dare," Henby went on. "I think you ought to know that for some time he has been blackmailing Mrs Riddel."

"Oh," said Roger. "Dangerous occupation."

"There are times when I know people would gladly murder me for being flippant," said Henby, with another grin. "I also know I ask for it, West, but this is serious. O'Dare has been blackmailing Cyn—Mrs Riddel."

"Oh, call her Cynthia," invited Roger. "Everyone in London knows that you were and perhaps still are on good terms with her, so you won't be giving anything away. When did you learn about this blackmailing?"

"This morning."

"It's a pity Mrs Riddel didn't confide in us before."

"No one would confide in the police about a thing like that. You know very well why she didn't. I don't know what he had against her, but I'm quite prepared to believe her story. There's one thing which had better be cleared up now, too. At the beginning of the affair, when you first came to see me, I told you that Riddel suspected Cynthia of having an affair—with me. It wasn't so, but I knew you would probably find out, and got it off my chest."

"Even from my bed, I can tell you that it's useless to come here and tell me half a story. If Mrs Riddel was being blackmailed, I want to know why."

"I can't make her tell me that," Henby declared.

"Something wrong with the staff work?" asked Roger.

Henby said, in a sharp voice: "West, I came to tell you this because I thought it would be safe to do so. You aren't an official, first, last and always. You can see how an affair like this can effect a woman. I don't want her interviewed by heavy-handed policemen who will worry

the life out of her to get more information. The fact is
that she was being blackmailed. That ought to be good
enough for a start."

"It's woolly reasoning," Roger commented. "And, of
course, I must report it to the Yard."

"You can suggest to the others a way of handling the
situation," Henby told him.

"I suppose so," admitted Roger. "They aren't bound
to act on my suggestions, you know. If you've an idea that
by telling me this you can save Mrs Riddel from interrogation, I'm afraid you're going to be disappointed."

"I wish I hadn't told you," Henby growled, at last. "I
thought you would be helpful."

"My job is to find out who murdered Riddel," Roger
said. "Nothing else is as important as that."

"You know who murdered Riddel. It was Tandy."

"He may have used the knife and the blunt instrument," admitted Roger, "but we don't know why it was
done, and we certainly don't know who paid Tandy to do
it. We've got to find out who."

"All right, if that's your attitude," snapped Henby.

He got up and went out of the room.

"What a conceited, domineering beast!" Janet burst out.

"Not quite," said Roger. "He's a nice chap, but a
bit spoiled and headstrong. He's worried about Mrs
Riddel. I wonder if she has been blackmailed."

"He wouldn't make that up," protested Janet.

"I wouldn't put anything past him," said Roger, "but
it's quite possible he has his own motives and is acting
upon these, believing himself justified. Of course, I might
be wrong and he may be at the back of the whole business
and be trying to side-track us." He narrowed his eyes.
"When you come to think of it, Henby isn't such a fool
that he thinks he could confide in me and persuade me
not to report his statement. He almost certainly knew
that by telling me he was telling the Yard. The rest was

window-dressing. Now, why does he want us to know that his Cynthia was being blackmailed?"

"I don't know," said Janet. "Darling, I'm feeling hungry and I think I'll go out and have some lunch. Is there anything you want me to get?"

"Cigarettes," said Roger, "and a huge bouquet of roses, please!"

It was pleasant on the balcony at Bognor. A special chair had been brought out for Roger and he was extremely comfortable.

Sloan was sending fully detailed reports daily, from London.

At first, Roger was too indifferent to read them closely, but with improving health his interest grew. Now and again he felt a guilty sense of satisfaction because his progress was so pleasantly slow.

"I'd rather have you away in one piece than here in several pieces," Janet said. "That's one of the troubles, darling, I'm never quite sure that you won't get seriously hurt. I hope they finish this miserable business before you get back. Pass me my dress, will you?" She put it on, and when her head reappeared through the neck, she added: "You hope that you can be in at the death, don't you?"

"Yes," murmured Roger. "It's a queer situation, Jan. I——"

He broke off at a tap at the door.

"Now who's here?" asked Janet. "Just a moment!" she called hastily, as the door began to open. "Roger, see who it is."

"What have you been up to?" came a sepulchral voice.

"Mark!" exclaimed Janet. "Oh, you can come in!"

"You being simply untidy and not in compromising circumstances," said Mark who came in, smiling.

"You seem in suspiciously good spirits," declared Janet.

"Oh, I am! Fully recovered from the bump over the head, buoyed up by glowing reports of Inspector West's health from everyone I see when I look in at the Yard, sunning myself in the approval of the Assistant Commissioner, for no known reason, and mildly amused because everyone on the case except Bill Sloan is going round muttering: 'We must finish this before West comes back, we must finish this before West comes back.' Eddie Day keeps prophesying that you will return and have all the luck, as usual, and the last time I saw Chatworth, he said: 'If you do go to Bognor, Lessing, you might see if West is likely to be back soon. I don't want to send for him if he's still under the weather; mind you, this is quite unofficial.'" Mark took out cigarettes. "Messages all duly delivered, can you two come and have dinner with me to-night?"

"We'd love to," said Janet.

"You'll have to cut Roger's meat up for him, I suppose," said Mark. "Best behaviour from both of you, please, I am bringing a most distinguished friend."

"Who?" demanded Roger and Janet in unison.

"I'll tell you at The George at eight o'clock," said Mark. "And as it's turned seven I'd better get a move on. Sorry about the suspense!"

"Two to one it's Chatworth," Roger said.

Mark grinned. "You'll see."

They reached the hotel at ten minutes to eight, speculating as to the identity of Mark's distinguished visitor. Waiting in the entrance hall, Janet was assessing the dresses and Roger the faces of the people when Roger stiffened. Janet, noticing this, said:

"Who is it?"

"Don't look now," said Roger, "but in the right-hand corner, sitting alone, is a demure young girl in apple-green. Fair hair, brushed on her shoulders." He paused. "See her?"

"Yes."

"That's the girl who was to meet O'Dare at eight o'clock," declared Roger. "The girl who made the appointment when she saw him in Grosvenor Square. According to Bill, she swore it was an innocent appointment. There's no proof to the contrary but she was among the crowd at the Swing Club, and——"

"What is she doing here?" demanded Janet.

"Exactly. I—well, that's incredible," exclaimed Roger, and began to stare without trying to disguise the fact.

Mark came striding into the hall and went straight to the girl in the green dress.

"I want you to meet Miss Mary Anson, Janet," said Mark, his eyes gleaming. "Mary, meet Inspector and Mrs West."

Mary Anson smiled at them both, and said to Roger: "I think I have seen you somewhere before, Inspector."

"Well, I do get about police courts and notorious clubs," retorted Roger.

The girl laughed. "I suppose I asked for that!"

"That's the worst of policemen," complained Mark, "they can never behave with ordinary discretion. Let's go in, or they'll have given someone else our table," He manoeuvred so that he went in with Janet and let Roger follow with Mary Anson. "One of the shocks of Roger's young life," he murmured.

"What a dear, loyal friend you are," cooed Janet.

"Oh, come! I wanted to spring it on them both," Mark retorted.

"She knew Roger perfectly well!"

"I didn't tell her," Mark declared. "She probably recognized him after the Swing Club." The head waiter had stopped at a table for four, and the others joined them. "Hallo, how are you old acquaintances getting on?" he demanded. "Exchanging childhood secrets? Now let me make a confession," he went on, as they sat down. "I wanted you two to meet, because Mary has quite a story to tell you, Roger. I forged an acquaintance with her, displaying my usual cunning. Then I began to ask crafty questions. Then she asked me whether I was not a friend of Inspector West." He grinned. "That dealt me a mortal blow, but of her own free will she told me what she knows of O'Dare."

"I don't know that it is much of a story," protested Mary Anson. "I know Pat O'Dare fairly well—at least, I thought I did! And whatever you may know about him, I like him."

"There is loyalty," murmured Mark.

"He's good fun," Mary continued, "and it's difficult to believe that he's a criminal, Inspector."

"Oh, let's be friendly. The Inspector's name is Roger," said Mark.

"Very well," said Mary, and the twinkle in her eyes proved that she was enjoying the situation. "If Mrs West doesn't mind."

"Janet," corrected Mark.

Her story did not help a great deal, but it was interesting. O'Dare and Mary Anson had known each other for some eighteen months. They had met at the Swing Club because, Mary admitted, she had passed through a phase when she had admired every man and woman who knew anything about politics and economics. These interests soon palled, but her friendship with O'Dare and others at the club continued. One of O'Dare's favourite themes was the villainy of certain politicians and employers. Frequently he had told her that he could break George Henby by saying only half of what he knew about him.

"Did he ever tell you the half?" Roger asked, quickly.
"No."

"Who else did O'Dare dislike?" asked Roger.

"Colonel Garner and Lord Plomley," said Mary. "In

fact he told me that he thought Henby was conspiring with them about something or other, and told me that he was watching their houses. He did on several days— sometimes I met him there before we went to lunch. He looked on it rather as a——"

"Lark," murmured Mark.

"Well, he did. Pat is thirty-one," went on Mary, "but he often behaves like a boy in his teens. He was serious enough about it but got a great kick out of what he called his detective work. He refused to let me help him because, he said, there was some possibility of danger. And as I'm not free much during the day, I didn't try to make him change his mind."

"You run a hat shop, don't you?" asked Roger, calling to mind Sloan's reports.

"I own a hat shop," corrected Mary.

"Oh, she's a bloated capitalist," grinned Mark. "She shouldn't be a member of the Swing Club, where only the poor but clever foregather."

Mary and Mark, thought Roger, were getting on remarkably well. They dominated the rest of the conversation, while Janet and Roger sat back, Janet enjoying the crowd, Roger weighing the girl's story. He had not yet asked her why she had not been equally frank with Sloan, for little of her association with O'Dare had been in the reports. But that matter could wait for the time being.

They were on the sands, later in the afternoon, when Bill Sloan's merry face and dark hair suddenly appeared out of nowhere. To ingratiate himself, he had bought a large bag of chocolates. Chatworth had sent him down, to compare notes with Roger.

"The facts as I see them are straightforward enough," Sloan said. "There's nothing wrong with the Swing Club as a club. O'Dare, the secretary fellow Johns and the other people we caught upstairs were in this business, but the club committee knew nothing about it. I don't think there's any doubt about that. O'Dare was undoubtedly the leader of the wrong 'uns, and there's a connection between him and Tandy."

"A clear one?" asked Roger, quickly.

"Yes. Both of the Tandy's and Harrison occasionally visited the club, ostensibly to sell liquor, actually to compare notes with O'Dare. O'Dare was sometimes seen at the circus, too—not as a performer, but some of the other side-show people thought he had some money in it. We're still trying to find him, of course.

"I fancy that Chatworth is a little uneasy," Sloan told him.

"He ought to be," said Roger. "We can't make a case against the Tandy's and the others without a motive. Or have you found a motive?" he demanded.

"That's the trouble," admitted Sloan. "We haven't."

Roger said: "Well, I think it would be crazy to take the men away from Grosvenor Square. Ask Chatworth to leave a man there for a bit longer. The excuse for leaving them can be that Garner and Plomley need police protection. Do you think Chatworth will be open to persuasion?" he added, hopefully.

"Probably."

"Good! Now, there's one thing remarkable for its absence in the reports," Roger went on. "A convincing statement from Cynthia Riddel after she had recovered from the business at the Swing Club. The only statement appears to be that O'Dare caught up with her in the street and by means of threats induced her to go with him first to Putney and then to the club. There must be something else to it."

"She swears there isn't," Sloan said. "Any ideas?"

"Nothing very clear-cut," Roger admitted.

It was remarkable, Roger reflected, how quickly the most sensational story was forgotten. The guilt of Tandy,

Harrison and the others seemed to be generally assumed. Only one newspaper kept comment on the case alive. Few Members of Parliament appeared to show much interest in it, although Ingleton tabled a question every week, asking the Home Secretary whether he could throw any further light on the murder of Jonathan Riddel. Each time the Home Secretary replied: "No, sir. The House will be informed at the earliest possible moment after information has been received." In the House, by general assent, another committee was elected to continue the work of the original one. Marriott, who would not be able to work for some time, was omitted; Henby and Garner were again members.

Roger had not seen Henby since the visit to the hospital.

Eddie Day, who came in late on Roger's first morning back there, looked across at the desk and said: "Back again, Handsome? You haven't half made a mess of this case."

"Have I?" murmured Roger.

"You know you have. It ought to have been finished weeks ago, that's what I say. I don't like it hanging on like this, I don't like it a bit, Handsome."

"I revel in it," said Roger, tartly.

"It's all very well for you, you never take anything to heart. If it was me, I wouldn't get a wink of sleep. I'd probably get a severe reprimand, too, instead of three weeks off." He sniffed. "That's the trouble here, favouritism."

"Eddie," said Roger, impatiently, "you're the most exasperating customer I've ever had to work with. One day I shall tell you exactly what I think about you. It won't be pleasant."

"You needn't get huffy," remonstrated Eddie. "I'm only trying to be helpful." He turned his attention to some forged cheques on his desk, and they worked for a while in silence. At last Eddie got up and stalked out of the room. Roger rubbed his chin ruefully, and ran through the correspondence on his desk. Most of it was about the case—report after report, none of them giving him the slightest help. Then he found a letter addressed: "Roger West, Esq., c/o New Scotland Yard, S.W.1." He opened it with quickening interest, and read:

Dear Mr West,

I would appreciate it if, at your convenience, you would call to see me.

Yours very truly,
Plomley.

"Well, well!" exclaimed Roger, and glanced at the date. "Written yesterday. Perhaps he wants to apologize for trying to throw me out!"

He spent the next half-hour studying all the reports on Plomley. There was only one thing which greatly interested him and he already knew a little about it: for some months past, Plomley had been in failing health. Not quite sixty years of age, he might easily be taken for nearly eighty.

"I think I'll go this morning," murmured Roger. He got up and hurried out. He told Sloan where he was going, and reached Plomley's house a little after eleven o'clock. Sale, the footman, admitted him, and he was shown into the morning-room, waited amid the shiny new furniture and once more felt that there was something artificial about this house.

The door opened, and he got up, expecting Plomley. Instead, Cynthia Riddel came into the room.

Chapter Sixteen

BLACKMAIL

S HE looked well in a black and white check tailored
suit. Her eyes had a healthy glow, and she was
smiling as she approached him.

"My father will be here soon," said Cynthia. "I will
ring for coffee." Sale came in almost at once. When he
had gone, she turned and looked at Roger intently, and
then said: "Mr West, it was only yesterday that I learned
how much I owed to you."

Roger pretended to be startled.

"I did not realize it was you who saved me from falling
out of the window," Cynthia said. "It is very difficult to
say 'thank you'. I do say it, with all my heart."

"Well, a job is a job, and I had three weeks unexpected
holiday," Roger told her. "It hasn't done me much good,
I'm afraid, I'm as much in the dark as ever."

"Aren't you satisfied that this man, Tandy, killed my
husband in order to steal those pearls?" she asked.

"No," said Roger. "Are you?"

After a pause, she said: "I wish I were. It would be
much happier for everyone if it were true. I am a little
frightened of what might be discovered. Does that surprise you?"

"No. Only your reticence surprises me."

"Reticence?"

"Yes. You could talk much more freely than you have
done. Probably you keep silent because you aren't convinced that what you know, or think you know, has anything to do with the murder. Whatever the reason, you
are making a great mistake."

She said: "Perhaps you are right. I think my father has
several things to say to you. Immediately I told him that

you had saved my life he——" she gave him a rather tantalizing smile—"he revised his original opinion of you! You greatly upset him when you first called."

"He greatly upset me!" retorted Roger.

"I think perhaps my father can give you information which will really help," Cynthia continued. "I do not think it is concerned with the murder. You will have to be the judge." She poured out the coffee, and as she handed him his cup, she added apropos of nothing, "You think I am very heartless, Mr West, don't you?"

"About what?" asked Roger, deliberately dense.

"My husband's death."

"Not everyone wears a heart on a sleeve," Roger answered.

The door opened abruptly, and Sale hurried in.

"What is it, Sale?" Mrs Riddel asked.

"His—his lordship isn't in his room, madam," Sale declared.

"He must be."

"But he isn't," Sale insisted. "I've looked in his room and his dressing-room. He just isn't there, madam. I haven't seen him since he asked me to tell you that he would not be more than five minutes. He—he isn't any-where in the house, madam."

Plomley's daughter hurried out of the room as Sale repeated: "He isn't, madam." Roger pushed past him and followed Cynthia up the stairs. She turned to look at him, but did not speak. She led the way into a large bedroom, which was empty, into a small dressing-room which led from it, then stood in the middle of the larger room, her hands clenched. "This is ridiculous, Mr West. He was just finishing dressing when you came. I was surprised that he kept you waiting for so long. I wonder——"

She broke off, and led the way across the landing to a study. It was the first really homely room that Roger had seen there. It was empty, and Cynthia said in a strained voice:

"He can't have gone out."

"I think I can check up on that," Roger said. He opened a window which overlooked the street. Winneger was standing not far away. He beckoned the man, and then hurried downstairs, meeting him in the porch. "Has anyone left the house since I arrived, Winneger?"

"Yes, sir," said Winneger. "His lordship."

"Are you sure?"

"Quite sure, sir. A car drew up, a Daimler. I saw his lordship step into it. I couldn't be mistaken."

"Did you take the Daimler's number?"

"Why, no," said Winneger. "I didn't know——"

"All right," said Roger. He turned back into the house, and met Cynthia at the foot of the stairs. "He left in a Daimler car," he said.

"I think it might have been Colonel Garner's car, sir, but I'm not sure. The Colonel wasn't driving, there was a chauffeur."

Roger turned to Cynthia: "Would he be likely to go out with Colonel Garner?"

"I can't believe he went out at all," said Cynthia. "He was most anxious to see you." She was less composed now. In fact, she was frightened, and watched Roger tensely as he went to the telephone and dialled Scotland Yard. He gave instructions crisply: a watch was to be kept for Lord Plomley and for Colonel Garner's car.

"I can't understand it," said Cynthia Riddel helplessly. "What could have made him go out?"

Roger looked at Sale. "Was there a telephone call after I arrived, Sale?"

"There was, sir. The telephone was switched through to his lordship's room. He answered it himself. It was only a few minutes after you arrived. I was on the way to tell his lordship. He called out to me when he had finished talking, but he did not ask me to go in and help him dress."

"Is that unusual?" asked Roger.

"These days, sir, it is most unusual," Sale told him.

Roger said: "It looks as if someone saw me coming and wanted to make sure that we did not meet. Where is the best place for us to talk, Mrs Riddel?"

She led him into the morning-room. Absently, she tasted the coffee, which was almost cold, and put it down again. All the time she avoided looking at Roger. The tension was rapidly increasing. Roger had no intention of easing it. Cynthia was keeping something back and she was really frightened. He might get her to talk now.

His face was hard and set as he said: "Mrs Riddel, do you know where your father has gone?"

"Of course not!"

"Have you any idea where he has gone?"

"No. I don't know—I don't know." She hesitated, and then burst out: "He isn't well, the slightest thing can upset him, and a threat might——"

"Threat?" Roger interrupted, sharply, and she drew back a pace. He watched her levelly and then went on: "Mrs Riddel, your father's health is remarkably puzzling. He fell ill, I believe, shortly after your marriage, and he has never been well since. Is that true?"

"Yes."

"Do you know what caused his illness?"

She did not answer.

Roger continued: "Mrs Riddel, you arranged for Mr Henby to tell me that you, personally, were being black-mailed by the man named O'Dare. You have never dis-closed the reason for that blackmail. I put it to you—you were never being blackmailed, but your father was; isn't that true?"

She stared at him for a long time, but did not answer.

Roger went on. "This may be desperately urgent. We don't know where your father has gone. It is possible that someone with undue influence over him compelled him to leave the house without seeing me. It is possible that someone living nearby saw me arrive and telephoned immediately. If that was a deliberate effort to prevent him from talking to me, he might never return."

"Please!"

Roger said roughly: "You have played with the police too long, Mrs Riddel. Was your father being blackmailed?"

After a long pause, she said: "Yes. Yes, he was." She put a hand to her forehead, and he could see her fingers were trembling. "Yes. I don't know why. I know that O'Dare was partly responsible for it."

"Why did you pretend that you were being blackmailed?"

She said: "I thought you would be bound to find out that one of us was being made—made to suffer so badly. I preferred you to think it was me."

"What made you think I should ever find out?" asked Roger.

She said: "The arrest of the man Tandy. He—he collected the money."

"From your father?"

"From me. I—I acted as go-between." She was talking very quickly, and had lost most of her colour. "I think Tandy was merely the messenger. I don't think he knew how much he collected. It must have been tens of thousands of pounds!"

"And you have no idea what influence was exerted?"

"None."

"Why did you tell Mr Henby to tell me that you were the victim?" demanded Roger.

"I was so sure Tandy would tell you that he came to me," Cynthia said. "I thought it would save my father some distress."

"Did Mr Henby know the truth?"

"No."

There, thought Roger, was the explanation of Henby's visit; Henby had believed, like her, that Tandy would tell the truth. The logic of what they had done was evident enough; what he had now to decide was whether she was still concealing anything.

"Do you think the brown-paper packet was a factor in the blackmailing?" he asked, and the question startled her.

"It might have been."

"So when you brought me the pearls, you were trying to fool me."

"I wanted to try to stop you from worrying my father," she prevaricated. "Is that so wrong?"

"It's always ill-advised to lie to the police," Roger said. "Are you telling the whole truth now? You didn't know what was in that packet?"

"No; that is the truth."

"And you have no idea what O'Dare has against your father?"

"No."

Roger said: "Mrs Riddel, on the day before he was murdered, that packet was on your husband's desk. I have a statement from Mr Henby to that effect. Did you know that?"

"Yes," she said. "Jonathan was helping father. He managed to get the packet, and everything seemed over then. Over!" she added, bitterly. "It had hardly begun."

"When your husband asked for police protection, was it because he knew he was in danger while looking for the packet?"

"I don't know," she said. "It might have been."

"You knew from the first that he had asked for police protection?"

"Yes. My husband was not normally secretive, but he kept much of this to himself. I think my father confided in him about the blackmail. He must have done, because I didn't tell him."

"I see," said Roger.

He didn't see; several puzzling features had now been explained, but he was still befogged and bewildered. Out of the fog one fact emerged: Cynthia Riddel was in genuine fear for her father.

"Mrs Riddel," Roger said, with brutal directness, "are you afraid that your father will be murdered?"

"Yes," she said. "I am terribly afraid."

Roger left Winneger inside the house, and hurried to the Yard. There was no news about Plomley, and Garner's Daimler had not been picked up. There was no reply from Garner's house when he telephoned, a fact which puzzled him; there should have been a servant on duty, even if Garner was out. He saw Chatworth, reported briefly, and then left again for Grosvenor Place, this time going to Garner's house.

Sloan was with Roger.

No one answered his ringing and knocking.

"I don't like it one little bit," said Roger. "I wonder if there's a window open."

He stopped abruptly.

There was a sound in the hall, a shuffling noise and something else: a man gasping for breath. They stood quite still. The sound ceased, but started again. Roger looked through the letter-box, but a piece of canvas on the inside prevented him from seeing into the hall.

"We'll break in, even if it means breaking a window," he declared.

All the windows were closed and latched. Roger bent his elbow, to crack it against the glass, but Sloan said: "Mind your bad arm!" pushed him aside and broke the glass for him. Jagged pieces flew in all directions, and the crash seemed very loud. Sloan put his hand inside the room, gingerly, stretching up for the catch. He got a grip on it, and a few moments afterwards the window was wide open and they were climbing through. Already a small crowd had collected in the street, and two uniformed police were approaching. One of them recognized Roger.

"Keep the crowd on the move," Roger ordered.

Sloan was already in the hall. When Roger reached it he saw Sloan on his knees beside a man whose head was battered, who was unconscious, and who had obviously tried to crawl to the front door. There was a trail of blood leading from the stairs and stains on each tread.

"Open the door and bellow for a doctor," Roger urged.

He hurried upstairs. That trail of blood told its own grim tale. It started from the door of a room on the right; Garner's library, Roger remembered, and pushed the door wider open and stepped inside.

Garner lay dead on the floor by his desk. The desk itself had been opened and papers were strewn all over it and about the floor. Those near Garner were stained with blood.

Roger went to the telephone, was about to dial the number and then stopped abruptly. Sloan came into the room. "Cover that telephone for prints," Roger said, "it's probably the one used by whoever spoke to Plomley; there'll be another downstairs." He hurried down to the hall, where a middle-aged doctor and two uniformed policemen were bending over the footman. Two strangers were at the front door, peering in. "Who the devil are you?" demanded Roger. "This isn't a peep-show."

"*Daily Record*," said one man.

Roger said: "Well, you haven't lost much time. I can't spare you a moment for half an hour, but I'll gladly see you then."

"Thanks," said one, and added: "Peter, hop off and telephone Andy. I'll stick around."

Roger was already telephoning from the drawing-room. He told the Yard to redouble its efforts to find Plomley and Garner's car, then had a word with Chatworth and gave him the bare outlines. Chatworth's manner indicated that beyond causing further sensation in the newspapers, it would not help the Yard.

Roger rang off. Sloan was coming down the stairs.

"Send for Cynthia Riddel," Roger said. "Don't tell her what's happened, just say I must see her here." He dialled another number, and when it was answered, said: "Ask Mr Henby to speak to me, please."

"I think Mr Henby is in committee, sir."

"This is Chief Inspector West of Scotland Yard," said Roger. "It is extremely urgent. Interrupt him, if necessary."

"Very good, sir." Roger waited for some time, trying to sort out the confusion of his thoughts. Why kill Garner? Now the only one of the original members of the select committee who had not been attacked was Henby. What a business!

"What is it, West?" Henby came on the line, and he sounded distant. "I am extremely busy, and——"

Roger said: "I would like you to come to Colonel Garner's house immediately, please. Garner has been injured."

After a pause, Henby said: "Is he seriously hurt?"

"Yes."

"I'll come," said Henby.

By then, other men had arrived from the Yard, photographs were being taken of the trail of blood, of both bodies and the library from all angles. A thin, miserable-looking man was bending over the telephone in the study. Roger watched him for a few moments. A light grey powder was spread over the instrument, but there were obvious signs of finger-prints.

"It's been wiped over, has it?" asked Roger.

"Aye." The miserable-looking man lifted the instrument carefully until it was above his head, and then peered at the receiver. "Aye," he repeated. "A careless fool he was, tae. Lookit, Inspector, there's a beauty!"

He lifted the receiver off, and turned it upside-down. Close to the mouthpiece was a single finger-print in the powder, and a few smears on either side.

"Richt index finger, I'm thinking," said the Scotsman. "Aye, it's a real beauty, Inspector, I never want to see a better. The man must hae been in a michty hurry. Wheer's Morgan—Morgan come here wi' your camera, man, ye can do some useful worrk."

"So we've got a break this time," Roger said with satisfaction. "Get it checked with the files as soon as you can, McPherson. I'll be in for a report early this afternoon."

"Richt ye are, sir!"

Sloan came up. "She's coming," he said. "Any luck, Roger?"

"What McPherson calls a beauty," said Roger. "I think we shall get something from this. I've a really ticklish job for you, Bill. Find out whether Henby has been at the House of Commons all the morning."

Henby arrived soon afterwards. The police would not allow him upstairs until Roger had given permission, and Roger went down to join him. He looked well groomed and more angry than anxious, perhaps because of a sharp exchange of words with the sergeant on duty. He greeted Roger mildly enough, however. Then:

"How is he?"

"Dead," said Roger.

"Dead!" Henby drew back. "By God, this will cause a riot!"

"It's going to cause more than a riot," said Roger. "It's going to upset all our ideas about the case. This was done in the same way as Riddel's murder, a savage attack with a blunt instrument. We thought we'd got Riddel's actual murderer. It doesn't look so certain now. Have you seen Mrs Riddel lately?"

"I saw her last night."

"Her father is missing," Roger said.

"Plomley?" Henby was sceptical. "He hardly leaves his room."

"Well, he's missing," repeated Roger. "Mrs Riddel will be here in a few minutes. She ought to be here now," he added, looking out into the street. "I'd almost forgotten her."

Henby said: "Are you suggesting that anything may have happened to Cynthia?"

"Oh, no. I left a man with her. I——"

"Your men haven't saved the others from murder," snapped Henby. He swung out of the room and hurried into the street. His long strides covered the distance between the two houses in double-quick time, and Roger watched him disappear into Plomley's house. Roger telephoned there, and asked Sale whether Mrs Riddel had left.

"She was about to leave when Mr Henby called, sir."

They hurried in. The glow was back in Cynthia Riddel's eyes; obviously Henby's influence over her was both soothing and stimulating.

"Do you know what has happened to Lord Plomley, West?" Henby demanded.

"I hope to have some news of him soon. This might be it," Roger added, as the telephone rang.

Abbott's cold voice sounded at the other end of the line.

"This is Superintendent Abbott, West," Abbott announced. "You asked for information about Colonel Garner's car. It has been found. Lord Plomley is not in it."

Chapter Seventeen

BAD NEWS FOR HENBY

COLONEL GARNER'S car had been found abandoned in a narrow turning off Fulham Road. It was already being checked for finger-prints, Abbott told Roger, and he then asked what was happening at Grosvenor Place. It was ten minutes before Roger finished the story. Henby and Cynthia stood watching him, waiting: was it good news or bad?

Then Roger said slowly: "We've found the empty car."

"You must find Plomley!" Henby said.

"We're just as anxious to find him as you are," Roger said, heavily. "Mrs Riddel, you thought that he was going to give me some important information. Can you give me any indication at all of its content?"

In a low voice, she said: "None."

Henby gripped her hand.

"He'll be found," he reassured her. "Nothing must be left undone, West."

"Oh, don't talk like a back-bencher," snapped Roger.

He deliberately tried to make Henby angry, but was disappointed.

Henby went off with Cynthia Riddel, and Roger went to see Chatworth, but there was no news. He was in the A.C.'s office when Joe Forbes of finger-prints came in carrying several loose papers, all of them covered with large finger-prints—black smudges which looked bigger than life-size, although some of them were quite small.

"Have you got them, Forbes?" asked Chatworth.

Forbes answered with evident satisfaction: "The print on the telephone and three found on the steering wheel of the Daimler are the same, sir." He put two of the sheets down in front of Chatworth, pointed, and went into some detail about loops and whorls and scars. Roger leaned forward to watch him, even Abbott showed some interest. "Both times the man was careful up to a point. The dashboard and steering wheel of the car were wiped, like the telephone, but he left just enough behind. There isn't any doubt about the finger-prints being identical on all three things, is there, sir?"

"No," said Chatworth. "Is he on our records?"

"Yes and no, sir," said Forbes.

Chatworth glared. "What do you mean, yes and no? Either he is or he isn't."

Forbes was poker-faced, but Roger knew that he was enjoying himself. Forbes always behaved like a fool when he had something sensational to divulge.

"He isn't a man with a police record," Forbes said, "but we have got his prints, thanks to Chief Inspector West, sir, who gave me a card with them on some weeks ago. One of the men involved, as you might expect, sir. They are Mr Henby's finger-prints."

Forbes, his bombshell delivered, took his leave. Chatworth stared down at the papers in front of him. Abbott, for once, was restive; Abbott was a man who would be horrified if a Member of Parliament were proved to be associated with murder. Glancing at him, Roger could almost feel that he himself were to blame for discovering the print on the telephone and for getting a set of Henby's. Chatworth was deliberating, playing for time, perhaps.

Roger watched them both in turn, wondering what they would say if they could read his thoughts.

Chatworth said: "Well, that looks conclusive."

"Henby hasn't been at the House long this morning," Roger told him. "He was out during the murder at Grosvenor Place."

"As I say," repeated Chatworth, "it looks damning. Eh, Abbott?"

"Yes." Abbott seemed to sigh.

"Any objections, West?" asked Chatworth.

Roger said: "Not yet, sir."

"What do you mean, not yet?"

Roger smiled. "Henby might have an alibi for the time of the murder which would be proof that he wasn't at Grosvenor Place this morning. Then I should be full of complaints."

Chatworth tapped the prints.

"No alibi can answer those."

"I don't agree, sir."

"Kindly elaborate your theory." Chatworth was looking at him angrily.

Roger said: "Well, sir, supposing Henby used that telephone before this morning, and supposing he drove the Daimler yesterday? We have to prove that the prints were made about the time of Garner's murder and Lord Plomley's disappearance. An alibi, even a poor one, would give us plenty to do. Mind you, sir, I accept the reasonable theory, that Henby probably made the prints this morning."

"I was hoping you were going to be reasonable," said Chatworth. "Well, it's a nasty business. The newspapers mustn't get hold of this until it's absolutely conclusive. I'd better see Henby myself," he added.

Roger murmured: "Would a word with the Home Secretary first be advisable, do you think?"

"Yes, perhaps it would."

"And I think Henby would gladly come and have a word with me without being fetched," Roger went on. "If he comes into the Yard unescorted, it will arouse less comment than if I went out for him. Sloan himself is watching him, sir, I don't think there is any chance that he will get away."

"I hope not," said Chatworth. "All right, West." He nodded as Roger got up to go. "Don't tell Sloan, don't tell anyone until we're absolutely certain of our ground," Chatworth ordered. "Be careful what you say to Mrs Riddel, too. She's in the waiting-room."

"Sorry to have kept you so long," Roger said when he saw her. "Please sit down."

"I am tired of sitting," she said. "Have you found my father?"

"Not yet," admitted Roger. "I take it that you realize

that the most important unknown factor is simply: what secret knowledge of your father's life enabled the blackmailer to exert such influence over him?"

"I have already told you that I have no idea."

"Do you think it probable that it was connected with matters likely to be investigated by the select committee?"

"When I say that I have no idea, I mean that I know nothing," she retorted sharply.

Roger sat on the corner of a table. "Your father has suffered for months, perhaps for years. His life has been made miserable; so has yours. Your husband has been murdered, Colonel Garner has been murdered, Mr Marriott and Garner's footman have been seriously injured. There is no way of telling how far this might spread and how many men might be killed or maimed for life as a result of it. If you have any indication of the nature of the secret, you must tell me now. If you don't you cannot evade responsibility for whatever may follow."

She said, almost too quickly: "I have nothing to add."

Roger asked: "Did your husband know the secret, Mrs Riddel?"

"I don't know."

"Do you think he did?"

"You have reminded me of the seriousness of the situation," she flashed. "It is too serious for me to indulge in guesses or for you to try to work on opinions."

Roger gave in: "Very good, Mrs Riddel. I hope you won't find it necessary to leave town for a few days."

He watched her leave, her head held high, and when she turned into Cannon Row, he walked after her.

She went into the House of Commons.

"So she wants to talk to her George," murmured Roger.

Chatworth sent for him as soon as he got back to his office. Chatworth had spoken to the Home Secretary. The situation was to be handled with the utmost discretion, naturally. West was to ask Henby to call and see him at once.

Roger said: "If he can't explain his movements this morning, what will you do, sir?"

"What can we do?" demanded Chatworth. "We'll have to arrest him."

"And then we'd have to charge him, even if it were only to apply for a remand while we kept him in custody," Roger pointed out. "Don't you think we could serve our purpose better by letting him stay free for a while? He can be watched closely enough. I could get his statement about his actions this morning and have the situation established. If he has an alibi, we could work on breaking it, of course. I can't see that it's necessary to arrest him at once. A few days won't make any difference."

Chatworth said: "West, don't you think Henby is guilty?"

"I think if we act too soon he might get away with it," declared Roger, "and we don't want any mistakes now, do we?"

"No. No, I suppose not. All right! Talk to him. Let me know what he says. Oh—what happened with Mrs Riddel?"

"Very little, sir, I'm afraid," said Roger. "I've let her go, but warned her to stay within call. I——"

He broke off, for there were hurried footsteps outside. Few people approached Chatworth's office in such haste; the door was thrust open, and into the room strode Mark Lessing. It was unheard of, a major offence.

Roger began: "Look here, Mark——"

"Oh, permit Mr Lessing to address us," said Chatworth, oozing sarcasm. "It is customary for callers to knock, even those who have not asked permission to enter this office, but then, we all know your remarkable enthusiasm."

Mark grinned. "I'm so full of it that I came in without

thinking, Sir Guy—sorry. I wanted Roger, really. I think I can take him to Patrick O'Dare."

Chapter Eighteen

O'DARE

ROGER'S car wove in and out of the traffic. He turned out of Coventry Street, went across Shaftesbury Avenue, drove along quiet back streets until he was in Marylebone, past Lord's out towards West Hampstead. Behind him was a second car with Winneger, another sergeant and two detective officers; all of them were armed.

Mark elaborated the story which he had told to Chatworth while Roger was making arrangements for the journey.

"Mary Anson did the trick, Roger. She had a message from O'Dare and sent me word immediately," he finished. "I tried to telephone you, but they couldn't find you and I thought it would be as quick if I came along. We've got to be careful. Mary's gone to this place."

O'Dare had given Mary Anson an address in West Hampstead; he had told her in the message that it was a few minutes' walk from the bus terminus. It was Number 8, Well Street. The Hampstead Police were already watching the street.

"I suppose you can trust her," Roger said, at last.

"I don't think there's any doubt at all," answered Mark. "What point would there be in sending us in force to a false address? I told her to wait at the end of Well Street."

"First right, first left and right again, isn't it?"

"Yes, according to your map."

Roger slowed down now. There she was, standing near a pillar-box. Her suit was almost the same colour as the box. She looked distinctive, and she wore no hat; Roger had never seen her with a hat, nor seen her hair untidy.

She looked hard at the car, and then her expression brightened and she waved to them. Two plain-clothes men from the Hampstead Division were in sight, one of them in the porch of a house from which he could see the whole length of Well Street, which was a short, narrow thoroughfare, with tall terrace houses on either side.

Roger pulled up, and the other car stopped behind him. Mark jumped out, and smiled broadly:

"We weren't long, were we?"

"A miracle of speed," admitted Mary, looking at Roger. "I've only been here a few minutes, darling." That "darling" brought Roger up with a start. It was not casual, there was feeling in it. He saw Mark grip her hand for a moment, and then she asked: "Are you going to do the same as you did at the club, Inspector?"

"More or less," said Roger.

"I hope you won't get hurt again," murmured Mary. "I suppose Mark has told you that I am to go straight in, tap at the door of Room 5 and ask for Mr Ireland."

"Yes."

"Do you want me to go?" asked Mary.

"No," said Roger, "there's no need for you to stick your head in a noose."

"I've no objection to helping," she said, without enthusiasm.

"I thought you liked O'Dare."

"That was before I read the full details of what happened to Colonel Garner."

"I see," said Roger. "I don't think I'll ask you to go along, all the same." He broke off when a Hampstead inspector came up. "Hallo, Inspector. Sorry to start trouble in your beat."

"Don't mind me." The Hampstead man was tall, heavily-built, with a dark jowl and attractive blue eyes. "You're after this O'Dare fellow, aren't you? I hope you get the devil. Well, I've something for you. The house is a rooming-house. We inspect the register regularly, and there's been no trouble of any kind. Clean, respectable, run by an elderly couple who get their living from it. The old man was in the High Street after I got your message, and I've had a word with him. There was a man named Ireland who came on the night of the Swing Club raid. Late at night, in fact. Some things don't tie up, though. This Ireland has dark hair and the description differs very much from the one you circulated of O'Dare. Of course, disguise might answer that," he admitted. "Ireland hasn't been out a great deal, and spends most of his time reading. They get his breakfast and lunch, he goes out for dinner or else has a snack in his room. He's stayed here once or twice before, but this is his longest visit."

"Does he have visitors?" asked Roger.

"Not many," said the Hampstead man, "but he's got one now. At least, he had just before the old man left, and my fellows have been watching the house since. They've seen no one come out."

"Nice work," said Roger.

"I'll ask one favour," said the Hampstead man. "Let me come with you when you start."

Roger laughed. "That's fair enough, if you don't mind risking your neck. If we walk on the same side as Number 8, they won't be able to see us from the windows, and the door will probably be open."

"The street door is open," the Hampstead man told him, "and I've got a key to Room 5."

"I'll send one of my men to every point of vantage, and then we'll close in," said Roger. He gave Winneger instructions and, when that was finished, looked at Mark. "I suppose you want to be in on this?"

"I should think so!"

Roger thought that the girl looked anxious, but she made no protest. They crossed the end of the street, for the even numbers were on the opposite side, and then

Roger, the Hampstead Inspector and Mark turned into the street.

They had passed several houses when a man came out of Number 8. He did not look towards them, but hurried in the opposite direction. He was a short, plump man, and there was something about him which Roger thought was familiar.

"They'll stop him at the other end," said the Hampstead man.

"Good," said Roger. "I——"

He stopped as the man turned suddenly, and hurried back towards the house. It looked as if he had forgotten something. He did not glance at Roger, but averted his eyes as he drew near Number 8. Roger stood quite still, and put out a hand to detain the others.

"D'you know him?" asked Mark.

"That is Mr Ingleton, M.P.," said Roger, softly.

It was impossible to tell whether Ingleton knew they were there. He was hurrying, and at that distance he looked like a man greatly worried. He turned into the gateway of Number 8, and hurried up the short flight of steps.

The Hampstead man said: "He might have noticed something and gone back to warn Ireland."

"There's nothing we can do about that," said Roger, "and we've got the key." He moved off again, and was the first to walk up the steps. The house was quiet, and for a moment they stood in a gloomy hall. Suddenly a door opened upstairs, and there were footsteps on the landing. Roger felt sure it was Ingleton. They saw his feet and legs as he hurried down, and all stepped hastily into a room on the right. Ingleton did not appear to know that anyone was there until Roger whispered:

"Just a moment, please!"

Ingleton turned sharply on his heel. Roger shot out his hand and thrust a handkerchief over Ingleton's mouth and nose. Mark lifted Ingleton clear of the ground and carried him into the front room, a gloomy parlour.

Roger did not think that Ingleton had recognised him, but he took no chances. He signalled to Mark to look after the M.P., then stepped into the passage with the Hampstead inspector. His thoughts were chaotic; the appearance of Ingleton had been a shock. He went up-stairs steadily enough, however, with the Hampstead man on his heels. Roger reflected, gratefully, that the inspector had not asked a single question; the man was efficient beyond the average.

They reached the landing.

"A room on the right," the Hampstead man said.

The landing was poorly lit, the only light coming from a frosted window above the stairs. Tall pieces of furniture were against the walls, and there were several chairs. The bathroom door stood open. There was complete silence. Mark was doing a good job.

"Open the door," Roger whispered.

The Hampstead man inserted the key, turned it, then as softly turned the handle. There was a faint squeak. The Hampstead man waited, but there was no sign that the squeak had been heard. He glanced at Roger, who whis-pered:

"Throw it open."

As it swung open, Roger stepped inside. He moved swiftly and kept his hand in his pocket, on the gun. "Ireland" was sitting at a table near the window, with his head in his hands, and a book open in front of him. Not until the door crashed back against the wall did he realize that anyone had entered. Then he jumped up, sending his chair backwards.

"Stay where you are," Roger snapped.

"Ireland" gaped at him.

If he were O'Dare it was a miracle of disguise. His dark hair was not the only change; his skin looked darker, he was poorly dressed, he looked rather a weedy man of middle age, not a spritely youngster like the fair-haired O'Dare.

"Who—who are you?" The question came in a reedy voice.

"I am a police officer," said Roger. "Patrick O'Dare, it is my duty to charge you with complicity in the murder of Colonel Randolph Garner, and I warn you that anything you say may be used in evidence."

"Ireland" did not speak.

Roger said: "Let's get him to the Yard."

It had been remarkably easy, too easy, compared with all that had happened before on this case. He was glad when he reached the street and was able to study the man more closely and in a better light. Now, for the first time, he saw that the face had been stained; there were lighter patches under the ears. He eased "Ireland's" collar away from his neck, and peered down; the skin beneath the line of the collar was much lighter. There were several patches of hair lighter at the roots than at the ends.

The Hampstead man marched "Ireland" off—a silent prisoner who had uttered no word except that reedy: "Who are you?" Was he O'Dare?

Roger re-entered the house and turned into the front room. There, Mark had pulled back the curtains, to let in the light. Ingleton was sitting on a horse-hair sofa, looking pale and harassed. Mark was leaning against the front of an upright piano.

Roger said: "Well, Mr Ingleton?"

"Hallo West," said Ingleton, in a low-pitched voice. "I suppose I have asked for trouble."

"I think you've got plenty," Roger said.

"I can explain everything, I think," said Ingleton, without confidence.

"I don't know that there will be much time," said Roger. "Had you been to see O'Dare?"

"O'Dare?" Ingleton looked startled. "I saw the man Ireland."

"His name is O'Dare."

Ingleton stared. "You can't seriously believe that, West! O'Dare is a fair-haired, young man. Ireland is—well, you've seen him yourself, haven't you?" When Roger did not answer, Ingleton went on: "That isn't O'Dare. I know O'Dare too well, I've known him for years at the Swing Club. You certainly can't accuse me of coming to see O'Dare."

Ingleton returned his gaze steadily. Mark swung his legs restlessly. Suddenly there were footsteps outside. The footsteps of a woman in a hurry. They turned into the gate, came up the steps, and as they reached the hall, Mary Anson called out:

"Mark, where are you?"

Roger called: "In here, Miss Anson. The door on the right."

She came hurrying in, a little out of breath. She ignored Ingleton and said to Roger:

"You don't think the man outside is O'Dare, do you?"

"Yes," said Roger.

"But you can't!" she protested. "He's nothing like O'Dare. The features aren't the same. O'Dare's eyes were blue, there just isn't any doubt about it, he's not O'Dare."

"That's what I've been trying to tell him," said Ingleton. "It's no use thinking that he's O'Dare, West."

The door of the room banged.

Roger, looking at Mary, saw it close, jumped towards it and nearly pushed her over. As he reached it he heard the key turn in the lock, outside. By then Mark was already at the window, and they could hear footsteps racing down the flight of steps to the pavement. Mark flung the window up. Roger swung himself out as a man sped past the house towards the far end of the street.

Chapter Nineteen

CHASE

ROGER reached the pavement twenty yards behind the
running man. Two or three policemen had already
turned in from the top end of the street and were running
fast, but Roger outdistanced them. He could see the
fugitive nearly at the corner, and he thought with relief
that his own and the Hampstead men were stationed there
in some force: there would be three men at least. He saw
two of them suddenly turn into the street.

The escaping man seemed to ignore them.

Roger did not know whether he was the real O'Dare
or not; he was dark-haired and he ran with the ease of a
young man in good condition. That was all he noticed as
the two men closed on him.

The fugitive swerved, and handed both men off.

It was brilliantly done. One moment there had seemed
to be no hope for him, the next, one man was on the
ground and the other reeling back, and O'Dare—this
must be O'Dare!—was racing towards the corner. Roger
was not much more than ten yards behind now. He heard
the thudding footsteps of the policemen who were coming
in support, and, glancing over his shoulder, saw Mark
following. Then he gave all his attention to the escaping
man. He just caught a glimpse of the third man—one of
the men from the Yard—closing with O'Dare—and then
the Yard man toppled over, and O'Dare raced towards the
corner.

They had lost him.

Roger opened the front door of his house, and stood
for a moment in the passage. He opened the door fully
and Janet jumped from her chair.

"Roger? You scared me."

He kissed her, and said: "That better? I want a whisky and soda, sweetheart. I'm not particular about the soda."

Janet said again: "Sit down, darling, I'll get it."

She returned to the kitchen in a few moments, a glass of whisky in her hand and the syphon in the other.

He was hungry; that was a good sign. Janet, who always cooked an evening meal, had only to serve it. He helped her to carry it into the dining-room.

"Well," said Roger, when they had finished and had washed up, "I've no one but myself to blame, if that's any consolation. I was completely taken in by a very neat trick." He told her what had happened, and went on: "O'Dare was obviously afraid that we would get on the trail of the man Ireland. He had one room at the house; he's used it on and off for years. The old couple who keep the place didn't dream we were looking for him. He called himself Smith," added Roger, ruefully. "He brought his friend and helpmate, Ireland, to draw our fire, and——"

"Wasn't that asking for trouble?" asked Janet. "To have him in the same house."

"Apparently Ireland was of some help to him and they had to compare notes," said Roger. "It wasn't safe, but it wasn't particularly dangerous. I think O'Dare lost his nerve when I actually went to the house. I wish he'd break his neck!"

"Have they found the car he stole?"

"Yes, on Hampstead Heath. All the proper things are being done," Roger went on, "and we may pick him up now he's really on the run, but——" he shrugged his shoulders. "It doesn't alter the fact that I had him in my hands and let him go."

"What about the man you did catch?" asked Janet.

"Strong and silent like the rest of them," said Roger, restlessly. "I'm beginning to think that their remarkable loyalty to O'Dare is the most astonishing thing of the

whole business. They just won't talk. I've had another go
at the Tandys, Harrison, Bray, the whole mob of them,
and I can't get a word out of them. This man Ireland is
just as bad."

"What about Ingleton?" asked Janet.

"There we are really in trouble," said Roger. "There's
no reason why he shouldn't have paid a call on Ireland.
We've nothing with which we can charge him. He gives
what seems to be a perfectly good reason for his call—
Ireland wrote to him and asked him to discuss certain
aspects of political economy in which Ingleton is interested. I can ask why Ingleton went to see him instead of
making the fellow do the travelling, but there's no reason
why Ingleton shouldn't go if he wanted to. In fact, the
only odd thing that happened with Ingleton is the way
he greeted me when I went in to see him. He expected
trouble. He knew that trouble was in the offing, and that
if O'Dare were caught he would have a hard job to
explain himself. Now he just puts a bold face on it, and
invites me to charge him with any offence. Of course, we
can't."

"And what about Henby?" asked Janet.

"He says that he was shopping this morning," Roger
told her, "and he gave us the names of several shops where
he called. He was certainly at two of them. It need not
have taken him long to get to Grosvenor Place, of course."

"Do you think Henby killed Garner?" Janet asked.

"I don't want to think so," admitted Roger, "but the
evidence piles up. I think Abbott is pressing for an arrest.
I'm under a cloud, and Chatworth might decide to go
ahead. If he does, it will be the sensation of a century!"

Janet said: "Well, put your slippers on and forget it
for an hour or two."

"Mark will be here about half-past eight," said Roger.
"Probably with his young woman. Yes, Janet, he is
serious this time. Sloan might look in, too." He stretched

himself and went on: "Four major mysteries: the packet; Henby and Cynthia; the murders; and Plomley. No trace of the old boy," he added, in a worried voice. "I hope we don't find the corpse."

"Would anyone kill the man they were blackmailing?"

"In some circumstances, yes," said Roger. "One good thing has come out of to-day's show. Henby, Ingleton, Cynthia and everyone who might be concerned are being really closely watched. And with the whole country looking for O'Dare and Plomley, something must break sooner or later."

He lay back in an easy chair facing the window, and dozed. Janet was busy in the kitchen.

A car drew up outside. He opened his eyes, and then sat up, for it was Mrs Riddel's Riley. He was standing in front of the fireplace when the front-door bell rang, and just missed seeing the caller, but the footsteps were not those of a woman. He decided to let Janet open the door, and she came hurrying along the passage.

Then Henby said: "Good evening. Is Inspector West in?"

Henby wore a well-fitting dinner-jacket, and he had recently had his hair cut. As he entered the room, Roger thought again how good-looking he was.

He did not offer to shake hands.

"Well, West?"

"Most informal," said Roger. "If you and Mrs Riddel make a habit of this, my Chief will begin to think that I'm in the conspiracy."

Henby laughed. "I don't think that greatly worries you! You've had quite a day, haven't you?"

"Too much of a day."

"I hope I can give you something to round it off nicely," said Henby, sitting down and accepting a cigarette. "I've just come from Ingleton, and he told me what happened at Hampstead. Too bad."

"For Ingleton?"

Henby said: "That's one of the things I want to talk to you about. Ingleton went to see this man Ireland on my behalf."

"Oh," said Roger, warily.

"And Ireland wrote to me—I had a note by hand—saying that he thought he could give me some information about Lord Plomley. I didn't want to get mixed up in it myself, if I could avoid it, and Ingleton offered to go along." Henby was smiling, but his voice was grave. "I hope that lets Ingleton out."

"Nothing lets anyone out, yet," said Roger. "Why must you keep playing the fool? If you had word about Plomley, your duty was to tell me about it."

"Duty?" echoed Henby. "It's an over-used word. I want to save old Plomley, you know. Not for his own sake, but for Cynthia's. You may as well know what the situation is—I've no doubt that you've guessed pretty closely."

Roger said: "George loves Cynthia."

Henby's eyes were hard.

"Yes. It isn't funny."

"No," admitted Roger. "Things like that aren't funny. They give you a very strong motive for murdering Riddel, I suppose you realize that?"

"Of course," said Henby. "But I didn't murder Riddel. I've wished I had the guts to. I've no love for Plomley, either. No man with any decency would put such a burden on his daughter. He's taken every advantage he could of her loyalty and her affection. He's made her life intolerable. If it weren't for her I'd never worry what was discovered about him."

"I see," said Roger. "You've let yourself in for plenty of trouble although you don't like him."

"Yes," said Henby. "Well, I'd better get down to brass tacks. You want to know why I've come, don't you?"

"Yes."

"To put my head into a noose," said Henby. "I was at Garner's house this morning. I slipped in the back way. O'Dare had telephoned me, and said that he wanted to talk to me there. O'Dare is the man who has been behind this from the start. I thought I might learn something useful. I found Garner dead and the footman badly injured, and I heard you knocking at the front door. Silly of me to run away, wasn't it?" He laughed again. "The truth is, I was scared out of my wits." He paused, while Roger contemplated him in silence.

"Well, what happens next?" demanded Henby.

Chapter Twenty

ARREST OF AN M.P.

ROGER said: "That isn't up to me." He went to the telephone and dialled Chatworth's private number. Chatworth himself answered. "It's West speaking, sir, from home. Mr Henby is with me, and has just told me that he went to Colonel Garner's house this morning, and found Garner dead. He panicked, and ran off. Now he's thought better of it."

"Do you say Henby is at your house!" demanded Chatworth.

"Listening to me at this moment, sir."

"Do you believe him?"

"I don't see any point in doing anything else," said Roger.

"I see," said Chatworth. "Charge him and take him to the Yard at once."

Roger replaced the receiver, turned and looked at Henby. He did not move or speak as Roger repeated the formula of arrest, but when it was over, he seemed to sag.

"We'd better get along," said Roger. He went to the

door. "Jan! I've got to go to the office; if Mark and Sloan come, tell them they'll find me there, will you?" Henby, a Member of Parliament, under a charge of murder, watched him without moving. Roger straightened his collar and tie, and Henby said with an edge to his voice:

"Can I give you a lift, Inspector?"

This was crazy! The man was driving himself to the police cells, had come with the full knowledge that it was likely to happen. There was no reason in it.

Henby drove steadily.

Roger said: "Does Mrs Riddel know that you visited me?"

"Yes."

"Have you seen her this evening?"

"Yes."

"Was this arranged between you?"

"I told her what I was going to do," said Henby, and laughed again. "It wasn't well received, but I'm tired of fooling about as you are. It's got to end some way. It can't go on like this."

They were in Victoria Street, driving slowly behind several buses. Twice Henby edged out to the middle of the road, but each time he was compelled to draw in again. Roger was trying to think clearly. They were within sight of Parliament Square when suddenly an idea came to him, and he said, abruptly:

"Pull into the kerb, Henby."

Henby said: "We're not at the Yard yet," but he obeyed and took a cigarette as soon as he had stopped. "Wouldn't it have done at the Yard?" he demanded.

Roger said: "No. Henby, if Mrs Riddel heard from O'Dare that her father would be killed unless you gave yourself up, would you be damned fool enough to do it?"

"I am all kinds of a damned fool," said Henby, "but not one as big as that."

"I wonder. Is that what happened?"

Henby met his gaze, and said: "I am tired of the whole business, tired of being suspected. I want it brought to a head. That's why I'm here with you."

"All right, let's get on," said Roger.

Henby let in the clutch, and something struck the windscreen. It splintered across and across, but did not break. Henby kept his hand on the gear-lever, staring at the white streaks, and Roger snapped:

"Duck."

He pushed Henby's head down and crouched down himself. There was another sharp sound. "Don't move," he said, and stretched out his left hand, to open the door. Traffic was passing, no one had noticed anything amiss; the shots were either fired from a silencer or an air-gun. Slugs could kill. The door opened. There was a sharp clanging sound as another missile hit either the door nearer Henby or the roof.

Henby was looking at him sideways.

"Be careful, West!"

Roger did not speak, but slid out on to the pavement, without raising his head. Passers-by stared at him in amazement. "Lie down on the seat," he ordered, and Henby obeyed. Roger peered over the side of the car, towards the opposite pavement. No one could have fired those shots while walking along the street, they must be coming from a window or——

Parked on the other side of the road was a stationary Morris car.

The clang of another slug or bullet sounded loud.

Roger said: "Keep down, Henby!" Roger reached the back and took out his automatic. He could see the man at the wheel of the Morris, and also someone sitting in the back.

"Police!" screamed a woman, when she saw Roger's gun, and a passer-by strode forward and knocked the gun aside. The driver of the Morris suddenly let in his

clutch and started off. Roger twisted round and snapped:
"I am the police!" Startled people made way for him,
but the Morris was a long way off by now. A uniformed
policeman came up. "Get over to the Yard at once and
put out a general call for a black or dark blue Morris,
number 4BC12."

Henby was lying face downwards across the two seats.
He did not move.

"Henby!" snapped Roger.

Still the man did not move. Roger got in, and eased
his head and shoulders up. He saw a thin trickle of blood
at the side of Henby's head. There was a wound on his
right temple. In a sudden panic, Roger thought: "They've
killed him!" He hardly knew what to do, but he forced
himself to keep calm so as to examine the wound more
closely. Then he felt Henby's pulse; it was beating.
Relief surged through him. "He's knocked out," he
muttered, and saw that the slug or bullet had caught
Henby a glancing blow, grazing the side of his head, but
not going deep; it was sufficient to knock him out at
once but no more. He slumped, took the wheel himself,
and reached Scotland Yard in two minutes. Men came
hurrying down from the hall, and Henby was carried
between them to the sick-bay.

In a quarter of an hour, he was sitting up and looking
blankly about him.

"You're all right," said Roger. "Don't worry about it."

"All right? Oh, yes, there was shooting, wasn't there?"

"Most of it was bad," said Roger. "I'm going to leave
you here, and when you're feeling up to it, send a man along
to see Sir Guy Chatworth—he'll be expecting to see you."

"Right," said Henby. "By George, I've got a head-
ache!"

"You're lucky you haven't got a coffin," said Roger.

"Where are you going?"

"To look for O'Dare."

He did not look for O'Dare, but hurried downstairs to the Riley and drove off, fear in his mind, fear for Cynthia Riddel. He reached the house in Grosvenor Place, and was glad to see that Winneger was on duty outside. There was, too, a man on duty at the back; surely no one could have forced an entry into the house without being seen?

"Anything to report?" he asked Winneger.

"Mr Henby left about an hour and a quarter ago, sir, that's all."

"No one gone in?"

"No one at all, sir."

He did not wait for Sale, but hurried into the room on the right of the hall. The light was on in one corner, and Cynthia was sitting on a settee, reading a magazine and smoking. She looked up, and he got the impression that her surprise was faked.

Roger said: "Well, I'm glad you're all right."

Her effort at pretence failed, she looked at him with unconcealed anxiety.

"O'Dare is still shooting," said Roger. "Mr Henby ——"

"No!"

"He's not badly hurt," Roger said. "That isn't O'Dare's fault. Mrs Riddel, why did he come to see me? Had he been told to do so on pain of some disclosure about your father?"

"George," she whispered. "Where is he?"

"Answer me."

"Yes—yes," she said. "I asked him not to come, but he insisted, he——"

Roger said: "What was the threat?"

"The usual threat," said Cynthia, wearily, "to disclose the truth, the truth I don't even know." She was standing quite still, her hands clenched by her sides.

"How was the message received?"

"By telephone. About seven o'clock this evening. It sounded like O'Dare's voice."

"Was it a long-distance call?"

"I don't think so, he spoke right away."

"And Henby was told to come to me and tell me that he was at Grosvenor Place this morning, or else the truth about your father would be disclosed. Is that it?"

"Yes, I've told you so."

"Was Henby at Grosvenor Place?"

"No," she said, quickly, "no, I'm sure he wasn't. He told me he wasn't. I should never have let him come to you, it was crazy, I am crazy." She caught her breath. "I hardly know what I'm doing or thinking," she said, "week after week, month after month, and I don't know why."

Roger said sharply: "Did O'Dare mention your father?" He went to a cabinet, which was open, and poured out a whisky and soda. He handed it to her, and repeated the question.

"No," she said, "my father wasn't mentioned. Thank you. You're not lying to me, are you? George isn't badly hurt?"

"He's probably talking to the Assistant Commissioner by now," said Roger. "Listen to me, Mrs Riddel. Henby's finger-prints were found on the telephone at Colonel Garner's house, and also on the steering-wheel of the Daimler car in which your father was driven away. That is conclusive evidence that he was at Garner's house this morning, that he telephoned your father. Do you see what that means? Henby is lying to you, Henby is black-mailing your father, Henby——"

She flung the whisky at him.

It splashed on his shoulder, and a few splashes touched his face and neck. The glass fell, with hardly a sound, on the thick carpet. She stood white-faced and with her eyes too bright, staring at him.

She turned away, abruptly, and raised her clenched hands.

"I'm not—sane," she said. "I'm sorry, I—I'm so terribly afraid you might be right. If you are—but why was he shot? Tell me that, why was he shot?" She turned round again, but now she looked a different woman, with hope reborn. "It can't be true if he was shot; you haven't lied to me about that, have you?"

"No," said Roger, "but——"

"Then it can't be true! It can't!" She was almost sobbing.

Roger said: "Why did you think it might be?"

"There's no need for me to answer that," she said, wildly. "There's no need——" She broke off, walked to a chair and dropped into it. "Practically every move I make is watched," she said. "I can't leave the house without it being known. But I was crazy to think George might be the blackmailer. It can't be, can it?"

"The finger-prints suggest that it is," said Roger. "The shooting to-night could have been staged deliberately, to make him look like a victim. He is the only one of the committee not attacked until now, you know."

"But wasn't he hit?"

"With a slug or bullet which did no serious injury," said Roger. If he could only confuse and muddle her, if he could only frighten her into telling everything she knew, it might be the end of the case. The blacker he made it against Henby, the more likely she was to talk. He went on: "There are other indications, Mrs Riddel. He once had the mysterious package, you know. It was stolen from me there, but there's no way of being sure. Possibly the man I thought had planted it had come to take it away. The thing that matters now is to find your father, to save his life. If O'Dare and Henby are working together, I can make Henby talk."

She said: "He wouldn't—harm—father."

"He told me to-night that he had no love for him," said Roger, quietly.

"But he couldn't——" She broke off, and he saw that she was shivering. He went to the cabinet and poured her out another drink, adding plenty of soda. She took it without a word. It helped to steady her, but her voice was husky when she went on: "It all started—everything started—after I broke off my engagement with George."

Roger did not speak.

"It was never announced. I broke if off because my father felt so strongly about it. That and—well, I wasn't sure of myself. There is something about George which is almost too overpowering. People do what he wants," said Cynthia. "He can make nearly everyone do what he wants. Had—had I married him then, it would have meant a complete break with my father; I weighed it up, I couldn't face it. Soon afterwards, father was black-mailed. I didn't know what was being used against him, I only knew that Tandy came and collected the money. I have told you that," she went on. "I didn't connect it with George, no one would have done. The blackmail continued. And I thought—I thought it was my husband."

Roger drew in his breath.

"Until the day he died, I thought it was he," said Cynthia. "I married him because my father wanted it, I always thought pressure was brought to bear on father. I thought it would be easier after that, but it grew worse, far worse. No one knows—what I suffered—with—my husband. The agony of living with him, the torment—if ever there was a devil it was Jonathan Riddel!"

She paused, but Roger did not speak.

"I was glad when he was killed," she said, abruptly. "And then—then I wondered if my father had hired men to kill him." She was talking in that same husky voice. "By then, I knew that everything that mattered was in the small packet. When I heard that Jonathan had come to see you, I thought he had brought the packet. I thought that he knew he would die, and wanted you to have all the evidence, so that he could continue to haunt my father even after his death. When I came, I realized you hadn't got the packet after all. I made up the story about the pearls. Everything became so hopelessly involved. I knew father would not arrange for Marriott to be shot unless—unless the worry had driven him mad. I suddenly thought that he might be trying to kill all the members of the select committee to keep his precious secret for a little while longer. I—I told George. He laughed it to scorn. He had already been helping, or telling me that he was helping my father. Then once—only once—I saw something in his eyes when father came into the room; it was hatred, I've never seen anything so naked, so malignant! From then on I became terribly afraid, and yet George convinced me that he was helping us. I believed him. I was never myself unless I was with him. I—I——"

She stopped, and looked at Roger.

"Now are you satisfied?" she asked, bitterly.

"Yes, quite satisfied," said Roger, gently. "There's just one other thing. This man O'Dare—did you know him before you met at the Swing Club?"

"I knew him as Preston. He worked for my father," she said. "He was a chemist at one of the factories. A small rubber factory at Slough. I rarely met him, but we were acquainted."

Roger said: "What's the name and address of the factory?"

"Plomex, Limited," she told him. "It's near the Trading Estate. Only in the last day or two have I realized that he might be concerned. He had some influence over my father. He is a clever chemist, specializing in rubber, and—but does it matter?"

"It won't be long now," said Roger. He went forward and deliberately took her hand. "I don't think George Henby guilty of anything but excessive loyalty," he said. "I hope to prove it."

Her grip tightened. "You're not just saying that to —to reassure me."

"I don't believe he is a murderer," Roger said, "although I am breaking all the regulations, but I think I can prove that I am right. There's one thing I want you to do. Stay here all night and if necessary all to-morrow. Don't go out. I shall allow no strangers in the house, in fact I may keep everyone out. Don't leave. If you disobey me, I can't answer for your safety."

She said: "I'll stay here."

Roger grew brisk.

"May I use the telephone? I want to take some men to the Plomex factory." He was dialling the Yard almost before he finished speaking.

Chapter Twenty-one

THE PLOMEX FACTORY

THE factory was a single-storey building, standing in its own grounds. It was near the railway and not far off the main road. Several street lamps were burning near it, but there were no lights in the building itself that were visible from outside. The wooden gates leading to it were closed, and as Roger sat in his own car, watching, young Hamilton climbed over the gate to open it from the inside. There were clanking sounds, as if he was having difficulty with a chain and bolts, but at last the gates began to open, and Hamilton stood blinking in the glare of the headlights.

He had brought Winneger, Sloan and several men with him, although he did not expect much trouble at the factory. It was unlikely that O'Dare would use it as a hiding place. Nevertheless, men were stationed about the wooden fence which surrounded it, and as he drove towards the main doors, they climbed over the fence and approached more closely.

When Roger switched off the engine there was no sound.

He rang a bell fitted into a wooden door. The front of the factory looked rather like a beach bungalow, and there was a verandah running round three sides of it. There was no answer, but as he waited, the headlights of a car shone into the drive.

"This should be the manager," Winneger said.

"Yes. There ought to be a night-watchman," said Roger.

He had sent Sloan to get the manager of Plomex, and Sloan and the man arrived while Roger was still waiting for an answer. The manager, a short, dapper man, now rather distressed and flustered, introduced himself as Mr Eustace Mortimer. He was angry. The night-watchman should have heard the bell; the man was intolerably lazy. Mr Mortimer opened the door and strode in, and as Roger followed he wondered if by any chance anything had happened to the man who should have been on duty.

An old man was standing in the doorway of an office, and he could not disguise the fact that he had been asleep. Bleary eyes from an unshaven face stared at the manager.

"I will see you in the morning," declared Mortimer.

Mr Mortimer led the way into a small but well-furnished office, and offered Roger whisky.

"Not now, thanks," said Roger.

"To business, eh, to business!" Mortimer had a sallow face and very bright eyes. "I quite understand, Inspector —you are an inspector, aren't you?"

"Chief Inspector West. There was a Mr Preston working here, I believe?"

"Oh, yes," said Mortimer. "Preston. Yes. He hasn't been in for some weeks. You won't find Preston here, Inspector."

"I'd like to know when he was here last," Roger said, "and I would like to see his laboratory."

"The laboratory," corrected Mortimer. "It is not

a large concern, you know. Mr Preston does not have a laboratory of his own. One small section is reserved for him." He led the way along a narrow passage, the wooden floorboards echoing under his feet, until they reached a locked door. Mortimer took out a large bunch of keys, selected one and unlocked the door.

"A great many poisonous chemicals are used here, Inspector: we take the greatest care of the laboratory," said Mortimer. "The windows are of toughened glass. That was done during the war, to make sure that no blast effect was injurious." He switched on a light. "It is a very fine laboratory for so small a factory, and, you see, everything is in perfect order."

It was a long, narrow room, with three sinks, benches, the usual paraphernalia—Bunsen burners, test-tubes, tiny weighing machines and glass cases filled with instruments; the walls were tiled. Everything was spick and span. By the side of each sink was a locker, and on one was the name: Mr Preston.

"Have you a key to that?" asked Roger.

"I fear not," said Mortimer, apologetically.

"It will have to be broken open," said Roger, and signed to Sloan. Mortimer looked shocked. "Before he went on holiday, did Mr Preston do a great deal of experimental work?"

"Oh, a very great deal," said Mortimer. Sloan put a small jemmy into the door of the locker, and there was a splintering sound. Mortimer winced. "He frequently returned here at night." The splintering sound was repeated. "Oh, dear!" exclaimed Mortimer, "is it really necessary, Inspector?"

"I'm afraid so," said Roger. "What kind of work did Mr Preston specialize in?"

"He had only one speciality: rubber," said Mortimer. "He applied for a number of patents; perhaps you are aware of that. Many were brilliant, quite brilliant. He was a man of ideas, too; he looked after what we call our mechanical goods."

"Mechanical goods?" echoed Roger.

"Small articles of manufacture," explained Mortimer. "Our chief work was, at one time, bicycle tyres and tubes, but during the war we did a great deal of moulding work for aeroplanes, mechanical goods, we always called them. Now, of course, we produce an infinite variety of domestic articles. There should be some samples here." He opened another locker, while Sloan was beginning to sweat, for the Preston locker was giving him unexpected trouble.

"Here, you see," said Mortimer, proudly.

There was great variety. Rubber rings, washers, handles, suède cleaners, buttons, pen-holders, hot-water bottles, stoppers, window and door wedges, finger-stalls, bathing-caps, tobacco-pouches, a miscellany of trivial oddments.

Mortimer was saying: "A separate mould is required for each one, of course. You know something about rubber manufacture, perhaps?" Roger shook his head. "The rubber itself is thinned in the mills," said Mortimer, "that is, a large machine rather like a huge mangle, then certain chemicals—powders—pigments is the word used in the industry, are mixed with the rubber to give it additional qualities. Different pigments go into different articles and, of course, there is the colouring pigment. Each batch, that is, every quantity of manufactured rubber ready for a certain special task, is carefully analysed in this laboratory. When it is approved, it is put into the moulds. These moulds, a mould for every article you see here, are subjected to tremendous heat," went on Mortimer. "I will not bore you with details, but the heat is really tremendous. Several thousand degrees. That is the process called curing. When the manufactured rubber is cured in the mould, nothing will alter its shape or size, nothing—except even greater heat, of course. If it were not so late, I would like to show you around, Inspector.

Mortimer was obviously an enthusiast on this subject.

"I may have to ask you to," said Roger, and looked at Sloan. "How's that going, old chap?"

"I think I've got it," said Sloan. He eased the jemmy in again, levered it, and then gasped: "Here it comes!" The locker door swung open.

At first sight there was nothing remarkable about the contents; Roger had already seen many of them before. He had each article taken out separately, however, and Sloan looked hard at him, as if wishing he would say what he expected to find. Roger, nursing a notion of his own, did not explain, but when he had handled each article, searched the locker again. He was beginning to feel disappointed.

He took out a small, sealed envelope, and started to open it.

"Really, these things are Mr Preston's private property," protested Mortimer.

"I'm sorry," said Roger. He took several slips of paper out of the envelope, and immediately he saw them his heart leapt.

Roger said: "I think we're all right. The cunning devil!" There were little heaps of what looked like waste rubber at the bottom of the locker, and he picked them up and examined each piece. Then he found one that was like a finger-stall. He examined it beneath the light, and he saw that it was grained, like the tips of a man's fingers.

Roger said: "Would it be possible to make a mould, Mr Mortimer, the exact shape of a man's fingers, fine enough to show the whorls and loops—I mean, the finger-prints—and to reproduce them?"

Mortimer stared at him. "Well, yes, possible. Blocks of remarkable fineness can be made by the electro-engraving process, but what practical use could be made of them? What industrial use would they serve?"

Roger said: "No industrial use, but they could hang a man." He examined the prints on the paper more closely, and added for Sloan's benefit: "These are Henby's. He didn't handle the telephone or the driving-wheel; the man who made those prints did them with finger-stalls like these."

"Good lord!" exclaimed Sloan. "Then Henby——"

"Henby is cleared. We want O'Dare and Plomley."

"*Lord* Plomley?" gasped Mortimer.

"Yes. He has been missing from his home since this morning," said Roger. "He hasn't been here, has he?"

"Oh, no," said Mortimer. He hesitated for a long time. Then: "No, but he telephoned me this evening, Inspector."

Roger snapped: "What did he want?"

"To tell you the truth, I am a little troubled about it," declared Mortimer. "He gave me instructions to draw two thousand pounds from the company's account to-morrow morning, and to take it to him."

"Take it where?" demanded Roger.

"He said that he would telephone me and tell me where to meet him in the morning," said Mortimer. "It is a most unusual request, but, after all, he is the Chairman of Directors, and I know that he has been unwell lately."

Roger said roughly: "Mr Mortimer, every evening paper has mentioned Lord Plomley's disappearance. Why didn't you get in touch with the police immediately?"

"Well, he *is* Lord Plomley," said Mortimer, miserably. "And also he *is* the Chairman of Directors. I felt that it was his business and he can do what he likes, can't he?"

Roger thought: "I must have you watched from now until Plomley's message comes through."

Roger was tired, but certainly not dissatisfied. If Plomley telephoned Mortimer in the morning to make an appointment, O'Dare might be with him; O'Dare might, in fact, collect the money instead of Plomley. There was another cause for satisfaction. Henby was free, no one knew that he had been under arrest. The quixotic false statement that he had been at Grosvenor Place would not carry any weight now.

Henby was now with Cynthia Riddel, with three policemen in the house as unofficial chaperones. Roger had not seen Cynthia since Henby had met her again. Chatworth wanted to know when Roger had first thought of the faked finger-prints.

Roger said: "When I knew that all the prints had been wiped off the telephone and the steering-wheel except these, I thought it odd, sir. It seemed more likely that the original prints had been wiped clean and faked prints made afterwards. That would only have been possible with something like this. I knew they would have to be made of rubber. The moment I knew O'Dare was a rubber chemist with a good practical knowledge, I thought I was getting somewhere."

As Roger sat up next morning and took a cup of tea from Janet a possibility did occur to him. He nearly upset the tea. He put the cup down and lifted the bed-side telephone and dialled Chatworth's private number. While waiting, he sipped his tea. "This will really shock the old boy!" he said, and chuckled with elation. "I didn't think—hallo, sir! It's West here."

"Good morning, West," said Chatworth, in a flat voice.

"It's only just occurred to me, sir, that two thousand pounds isn't much money on its own," said Roger, "but supposing Plomley has been told to instruct the managers of all his companies to do the same thing. He controls thirty or forty. There would be really big money in it. I'd like to check up with every company, sir, but it will use a great many men, and——"

"Get it done!" cried Chatworth.

Chapter Twenty-two

GRIST TO THE MILL

"BUT my dear chap!" cried Roger, in the middle of shaving, "anyone with an ounce of common sense in his noddle would see the importance of this!"

"S'ave," said Scoopy.

"Never mind shaving! I can't understand why I didn't think of it last night. Before last night. It must have been the enervating effect of Bognor. Or the bullet."

"S'ave," insisted Scoopy.

"You should never have let him see that brush," Janet called from the bedroom, "you'll never be able to shave in peace now."

"S'ave!" cried Scoopy, greatly encouraged.

From the nursery, Richard, who had been put back for a post-breakfast sleep, gurgled delightedly. Roger finished with his brush, put it down and looked for the razor. It was not in its usual place. Through the mirror he caught sight of Scoopy putting the shaving edge to his cheek.

Roger's heart leapt. "Here, you scamp! Give it to Daddy!" He rescued the razor, and Scoopy, just tall enough, snatched the lathery shaving brush and smothered his face. Roger grinned down at him, and started to shave in earnest, but he did not finish quickly. He was amused by the glow in his own eyes, and his lips kept breaking into a smile.

"Say fifty companies at £2,000 apiece," he told Scoopy, who was plying the shaving brush industriously, "and you have nearly a hundred thousand pounds, which is enough for anyone's birthday present. Our blackmailer meant to hold out until he could make a final coup, and this is undoubtedly it. Don't you think so, old son?"

Scoopy put down the brush, tip-toed to see himself in

the dressing-table mirror, grinned with great delight and said: "Ooooh!"

"I should think it is ooh!" Roger shaved the other cheek. "And oh and ah and um."

"Oh-ah-um," copied Scoopy. "S'ave."

"You've had your shave, and when you come to think of it, I had a close one," declared Roger. "All right, wait until I've done under my chin." He finished, put his razor safely out of Scoopy's reach, picked the child up and sat him on the side of the bed. With the handle of a tooth-brush, he took off the lather, while Scoopy leaned back ecstatically and closed his eyes. "There! Now perhaps you're prepared to give this matter of O'Dare and Plomley proper attention," said Roger. "O'Dare knew that he had the trump cards. He worked well, brought out his trumps, got Plomley away in what is called the nick of time, but don't let me catch you using clichés, young Martin."

Roger washed quickly, a bad example to his son.

As he dried himself, he said: "Now we can talk! What an idea. Blackmail through Plomley's various companies, and—ah! There's the snag." He looked quite crestfallen. "Yes, a serious snag. Supposing they are trying to get away with a couple of thousand from every company, surely one manager at least would tell us what is happening. They wouldn't all be spineless, like Mortimer. No. And O'Dare would think of that."

He hurried into the bedroom and, to Scoopy's delight, lifted the telephone. Then a man answered. "Is that Mr Mortimer?" asked Roger.

"Mr Eustace Mortimer speaking."

"Inspector West," said Roger. "You haven't had your instructions yet, I suppose? . . . No. Tell me, did you have any earlier instructions, a letter from Lord Plomley, for instance, telling you what to do in certain circumstances? . . . What? . . . Mr Mortimer," he went on, his voice hardening, "you have behaved most unwisely. That information should have been given to me last night."

"It has worried me very much," said Mortimer, nervously, "but it is from Lord Plomley, and the instructions were most precise . . . No, I haven't it with me, it is at the office, but I remember it clearly, Inspector. I was instructed not to be surprised if he telephoned me for a sum of money during the next few days; that I was to do exactly as I was told. What else could I do, Inspector? Even if his lordship was being blackmailed, I am his servant; a servant's first duty is to his employer. Yes, I will advise your assistant when I hear from his lordship."

Downstairs, at breakfast, Janet and Maude the help, a pleasant girl, were feeding the boys, Scoopy paused to grin, but tucked into his bacon and fried bread. Richard, his mouth open like a bird's, gurgled continuously until his mouth was filled, swallowed each spoonful with incredible haste and opened his mouth for more.

"How are things going?" asked Janet.

"Mortimer had a letter of instructions. The other people probably have one, too. I think there's a sound chance that I'm right," said Roger. "If anyone rings through when I'm gone, tell them I'll be at the Yard in ten minutes—er—twenty minutes, won't you?"

"Just drive off and break your neck," said Janet.

Roger kissed the top of her head.

"I'll be all right." He hurried out, and when he was getting the car out of the garage, he heard another pull up in the street. He looked round, and saw Mark's Lagonda.

"Coming," he called, and backed into Bell Street, guided by Mark.

"You look pleased," said Mark.

"I am. I think we've got something really useful." Roger gave a brief summary of his theory, but did not go into details. Mark drove behind him all the way to the Yard. When they reached the office, men were standing at every telephone. He went to his desk. There were several reports and he picked up the first and read it amid the steady hum of conversation, the ringing of telephone bells, the opening and closing of doors.

The report was brief, but Roger kept reading it, with an almost indecent satisfaction.

"William Hobjoy, manager of Pollex Ltd., boot and shoe manufacturers, Northampton, telephoned at 8.35 a.m. Yesterday received instructions to have ready £2,500 in £1 treasury notes for delivery in person to Lord Plomley or Lord Plomley's agent. W.H. warned to be ready for a journey."

Roger put it aside. The din was, if anything, worse. His smile widened, for there were seven other reports, similar to that on Hobjoy, concerning officials in companies belonging to one or other of the firms in the Plomley Trusts. In each, final instructions were still awaited. None were likely to be given before the banks opened, thought Roger.

The door opened, and Chatworth entered.

He appeared to be in an amiable mood. "Quite a hive of activity, isn't it? You certainly took me at my word. Are you making any progress?"

"We've had some difficulty in getting the names and private addresses of the managers," Roger said, "but we've done enough to show that Mortimer is one of many."

"Have we? You're doing quite well again, West, quite well." Chatworth gave Mark an almost imperceptible wink. "One might almost say very well."

"Another thing seems advisable, sir," suggested Roger. "Local police ought, in every case, to be asked to follow these managers. They may not all be sent to the same place. It means more telephoning, I'm afraid, and we can't get any more done in this office."

"And we shall drive the operators quite mad," said

Chatworth. "But it must be done. I'll send you con-
firmation in writing. Better get in touch with the Superintendent on duty in every town concerned. Don't go
through the Chief Constables, it will take too much time."
His voice was curiously flat again, it was almost as if he
had no heart for this business. "Report to me as soon as
anything develops."

Not once had the buzz of talk, the ringing and the
bustle of movement stopped. As a man obtained information from a company manager, he sat down, wrote a
brief report and brought it to Roger's desk. Then he went
back to the telephone. Reports were coming in more
quickly now. There were some from Manchester, one
as far north as Carlisle, several from Birmingham and the
Midlands, at least a dozen from London. The room grew
warm and filled with tobacco smoke, but the results which
were coming through kept everyone good-tempered.

At ten o'clock, there were over thirty reports.

"Well, we should hear from Mortimer soon," Mark
said.

"I hope he's not going to get bumped off," said a man,
passing over his report.

"Sloan will see to that," said Roger.

He felt misgivings, all the same. It was just possible
that he had been seen going to Slough, and that O'Dare
would try to prevent Mortimer from telling his story.
There was danger for the manager and danger for Sloan.
It was a nerve-wracking half an hour, made worse because
every inward call made Roger jump up, hoping that it
was from Mortimer or Sloan.

On the stroke of half past ten, Eddie Day came hurrying into the office, his eyes glowing with excitement.

"I say, 'Andsome! 'Andsome!" His shrill voice sounded
above all the others. "'Andsome, I think I've got it!" He
reached the desk panting. "I really think I've got something, 'Andsome. A fair-ground!"

"What!" asked Roger, startled.

"A fair-ground," repeated Eddie, eagerly. "Don't you see? It must be some kind of place where a lot of people wouldn't be noticed, that's obvious, isn't it? You ask yourself, isn't it obvious? It couldn't be at Piccadilly Circus or anywhere like that, either. I mean, even if twenty men were to come and give a packet of notes to another, the receiver would be snowed under, wouldn't he? So they must have somewhere to put it. And they must be somewhere where they wouldn't be noticed. Well, what about it, 'Andsome?"

"Go on," said Roger, tensely.

"I thought that would make you open your eyes," crowed Eddie. "You haven't got all the brain in this outfit, Handsome!" He had recovered his aspirate. "I thought to myself, look here, Tandy and his mob are mixed up in this thing, and they ran a fair or a circus, something like that. So I started from there. And then there's O'Dare. He's not an ordinary man, Handsome, he's a blinking acrobat, the way he climbs over roofs and gets about among traffic, not many men could do it. Acrobat—fair-ground! I'll bet you five bob these people are going to a fair-ground somewhere near London. It's Whitsun week-end, to-day's Saturday, there will be plenty about. Look how simple it would be! Go up to Madame Salome's tent, or something, she'd be a fortune-teller as well as O'Dare's agent, hand over the cash to her and then scram. Why, it's like falling off a horse. Perhaps it wouldn't be a fortune-teller, as we raid 'em sometimes," Eddie added reflectively. "It could be a strong man or a fat woman, or something like that. Well, what about it?"

"Eddie," said Roger, after a brief pause, "that's nothing short of genius. I must tell Chatworth at once."

"You'll tell him I thought of it, won't you?"

Roger laughed. "I will! And I'll never lose my temper with you again. A fair-ground, near London," he added.

"What's on? Eddie, hop along and see Parmitter, will you? He'll have a list of every licensed fair in the Greater London radius. And if you can find a telephone, get the local police near every fair-ground warned to stand by."

"Sure," said Eddie. "Okay, 'Andsome!"

He went out, strutting with delight.

"I think he's got it," declared Roger. "Wait for me, will you?" He hurried along to Chatworth's office, tapped and was told to enter.

Chatworth looked up, and said: "Well, Roger?"

"The news hasn't broken yet," said Roger, "but Eddie Day has had a brainwave, sir. I don't think there's any doubt about him being right. A fair-ground——"

Chatworth sat drumming his fingers on the desk and nodding. The telephone rang when Roger had nearly finished, but Chatworth ignored it. It rang again. Chatworth took off the receiver, said: "Hold on!" and continued to listen to Roger. Roger finished his summary of Eddie's bright idea, and also the outline of what he had arranged.

"Yes," said Chatworth. "It's a smart idea, I must tell Day so. There won't be a policeman left for traffic duty soon, though, we can't go on like this." He smiled weakly. Roger knew that in times of stress he was likely to make inane remarks. "Hal-lo!" boomed Chatworth, into the telephone. "Eh? . . . Yes, he is here. For you, West," he said.

Roger took the instrument.

"Hallo, there!" cried Bill Sloan, jubilantly. "Mortimer's got the cash and has had his instructions. You wouldn't guess where he's to report in a month of Sunday's. There's a fair opening to-day at Hampstead Heath, ready for the Bank Holiday week-end, and Mortimer has to report at the Ugly Woman booth. What about that, Roger?"

"A medal for you and a medal for Eddie Day," said Roger. He looked up, excitedly. "Hampstead Heath, sir! Day was right."

"That's good," said Chatworth. "Now all you have to do is to raid the booth. I wish it weren't Hampstead. It would have been easier in a small field, or—never mind, never mind! You won't keep the telephone inquiries going, will you?"

"There isn't much need," admitted Roger. "I don't know that I favour an immediate raid, though."

"What do you favour?" asked Chatworth.

Roger said: "It seems to me that a great number of the people working in the fair might be involved, and that we can easily run into a first-class riot once it's suspected that we're on the Heath in strength. We don't want a riot."

"We mustn't have one," said Chatworth.

"The only likely way of preventing one is to be there without being recognized at first glance," said Roger. "O'Dare and the fair people will expect the Hampstead police and a few special constables. They can all be briefed to watch the tent. Those of us who have worked on the case and might easily be recognized ought to use some kind of disguise, I think."

Chatworth frowned. "I'm never fond of make-up."

"Nor am I, in normal circumstances," admitted Roger, "but I don't see what else we can do this time. O'Dare will have spotters out. As soon as I turn up, or Sloan or Lessing or any of the others, word will reach him. He's got away too often for us to take chances. I think Day is right, he is an acrobat of sorts. And I'd like to make this arrest myself."

"I suppose so," said Chatworth.

"And there is something else, sir," continued Roger. "We don't yet know where Plomley is. We want him alive if we can get him. O'Dare might kill him, if he thinks the game is up. If it's possible, we've got to go in with a bang, and give O'Dare no time to think. One thing is fairly certain—he'll stay to collect as much as he can, and unless

he's warned that we are on the Heath, he'll go on col-
lecting. All the money messengers will be followed by
their local police, they can be checked without any
difficulty."

"Yes," said Chatworth. "All right, Roger, do your
play-acting. But make quite sure that no one from that
tent, not even the Ugly Woman, gets off the Heath. We
don't want O'Dare to make an escape while you're
dressing-up, you know."

"I couldn't agree more, sir," said Roger. "Is that all
for now?"

"Yes. Off with you! O'Dare will have made his arrangements for fleeing the country, and that mustn't happen—
it just mustn't happen."

"It won't," said Roger, confidently.

Ten minutes later the make-up expert at the Yard was
working on him, and theatrical experts had been called in
to work on others. Sloan came in from Slough, and waited
for "treatment".

Roger was out of the make-up room when the telephone
call came from the Hampstead police. The first three
people had gone to the Ugly Woman's tent, carrying
parcels; each had come out empty-handed.

Chapter Twenty-three

HAPPY HAMPSTEAD

THE fair was in full swing.

It was lunch time, and the crowd was getting thicker,
although school-children, mostly in parties, made up the
majority of the revellers. The "Caterpillar" and the
"Whirlwind" were screeching round, the swings were
busy, the coco-nut shies were thronged, roundabouts
were hurtling round with their horses bobbing up and
down. Hoop-la and skittles, Aunt Sally and rifle ranges

were doing good business. The sideshows were thronged, automatic machines were clicking over and raking in the money, the hoarse voices of the huskers were lost in the cacophony of steam engine, organ music, the crack of shots and the shrill laughter of the children.

Roger and Mark were together. Near them were Sloan and Winneger and several other men from the Yard, including Eddie Day. Eddie needed little disguise, he always looked more like the proprietor of a side-show than a Chief Inspector of Scotland Yard. He had been home and put on his loudest check suit, and he had a fake moustache; but nothing could make Eddie look more freakish than he did in real life.

Roger was grateful for the heavy clouds and threatening rain, which made the morning cool. Grease-paint and cheek-pads had altered his appearance so much that no one would have recognized him, although on close inspection it was obvious enough that he was disguised. He did not think that mattered. Mark, with dark beard and shaggy eyebrows, was dressed in borrowed naval uniform.

They made their way slowly and casually about the ground. Now and again they stopped to watch one of the side-shows.

The tent of the Ugly Woman was near the big round-abouts, they knew, with more space about it than most of the other tents. Strong men, palmists, clairvoyants, snake charmers, tipsters, sword swallowers and fire-eaters all competed for customers, boxers and all-in wrestlers challenged all-comers. Roger was quite sure they were not followed.

He felt an increasing sense of excitement.

"Eddie's the star of this case," Roger said. He looked at his watch. "Ten minutes to go."

"If O'Dare had suspected anything, he would have made a move by now," said Mark. "Don't fidget."

Roger grinned. "Sorry!" They were near the Ugly

Woman's tent, which was in full view. No one was inviting custom there but in the next three minutes two men entered, business men who looked out of place on the Heath. "Business is still good," went on Roger. "I— Great Scott!"

Mark stared. "Henby!"

"The fool," said Roger. "The utter fool. He——"

"Cynthia Riddel, too!" exclaimed Mark. "Weren't they being watched? Wasn't she told not to leave the house?"

"Yes, and warned of the danger, too," Roger said. "I'd like to bang their heads together! They ought to know that if they play the fool any more they're asking for more trouble."

"I'm still not too sure about them," Mark said.

They went a little closer. It was five minutes to two. Nothing now could delay the police raid, but if it happened when Henby and Cynthia were inside the tent, they would be in great danger. O'Dare would fight. Roger felt sure that O'Dare was there in person.

"Going in?" asked Mark, as they drew nearer.

"Not until our men show up," said Roger. He kept his eyes on his watch. "Four minutes. They might come out."

Two more minutes passed; a third. There was no sign of Henby or Cynthia. Roger, his satisfaction completely vanished, fussed and fidgeted. Then he saw the plain-clothes men closing on the tent. Several of them he recognized only from their clothes, others were badly disguised, but none of them who had played a prominent part in the case was recognizable. They were strolling in two's and three's. Roger's watch showed that it was two o'clock exactly. A dozen men looked at their watches at the same time, and then they started forward towards the tent.

"Come on!" said Roger.

He gave up all pretence, and rushed forward. He

reached the flap of the tent first, and pushed his way in. It was a large tent, partitioned, and the first space was only large enough for two people to stand: no one was there. He opened the next flap.

A sheet of flame rose up in front of his eyes, and he backed away, bumping into Mark. The inner tent caught alight as if soaked in petrol, and the roars as it went up deafened them. Roger and Mark struggled back, as the outer flap caught fire. They were hemmed in by plain-clothes men. The whole tent was in flames. Instinctively, the crowd rushed towards it; someone began to shout: "Fire, fire." The refrain was taken up, became a dull-throated roar: "Fire, fire, fire!"

The heat drove Roger and the others ten yards from the tent. Roger saw the C.I.D. men forming a cordon. They joined hands, keeping the crowd back, while the fire raged and fiery fragments flew through the air, dropping on nearby tents; smuts floated down and smoke rose high in the air.

"It's petrol," Roger muttered. He let the two men on either side of him and Mark link hands, and then hurried round with Mark, making a complete circuit, asking the same question: "Has anyone got out?" No one had been seen. "It can't end like this," Roger said. "Cynthia Riddel and Henby—there they are!"

The crowd let forth a terrific roar.

Henby came out of the flames, carrying Cynthia. She was a dead weight in his arms, and her skirt was alight; so was her hair. Roger tore off his coat and rushed towards them. Henby's clothes were smouldering, his hair singed and his face blackened, he was gasping for breath. Roger wrapped his coat round the woman's head. Henby croaked something, staggered and would have fallen had Mark not held him up. Other men broke through the cordon. A fire-bell clanged.

There was another roar from the crowd. It started on

the far side of the tent and was taken up on Roger's side.
Two St. John Ambulance men hurried up; Roger left
Henby to them and called Mark as he dashed to the other
side, where the crowd was still roaring. Two C.I.D. men
had been knocked down, and the crowd was seething with
excitement. Then it divided and Roger saw a man pushing
his way through and laying about him with a heavy club.
C.I.D. men rushed after him, but the crowd closed behind
him.

"That's O'Dare!" cried Mark.

Roger said bitterly: "We can't do a thing."

"Can't we?" Mark bellowed, in a voice which sounded
above the din. "Police, police! Make way!" He rushed
forward, forcing his way a few yards into the crowd.
Roger and the others followed elbowing right and left.
The crowd parted to let them through and then closed in
again. For a while they seemed hemmed in on all sides,
but Mark was pushing his way through wildly and, only
ten yards ahead, O'Dare—was it O'Dare?—was swinging
his club, and men were shouting, women screaming; from
somewhere a baby's cry was heard.

The crowd thinned out.

"There he is!" snapped Roger.

It looked like O'Dare, although his hair was dark. He
was still swinging the truncheon, but he had something
else in his hand now; an automatic. Roger thought: "He
mustn't use it!" At all costs he must not be allowed to
shoot in such a crowd.

Men were shouting: "There he is!" "That way!"
"Stop him!" The words meant nothing. Roger kept
O'Dare in sight, fearful lest he should use the gun. Then
someone jumped out of the crowd and drove his fist into
Roger's chin. Mark raised his arm and thrust the man
back, planting his foot in his stomach. Another man
rushed forward, swinging a stick.

"Here's the riot," Mark muttered.

There were several men among the crowd wielding sticks, shouting and swearing, marking down the C.I.D. men who now seemed to stand out clearly. Roger, his eyes watering from the blow, lost O'Dare for a few moments in watching the crowd ahead and in desperation leapt on to a hoop-la stall so that he could see above the heads of the throng.

He could not pick out O'Dare, but he saw something else which struck a cold chill through him. There were half a dozen fires about the fair-ground, tents blazing and smoke pouring upwards, as the sparks from the first fire took effect. People were panicking. He could see their faces, white and strained. The fire was spreading and the fight was getting out of control. The police could do nothing to prevent the panic. The crowd rushed in all directions and the hooligans laid about them, heedless of whom they were hitting now, intent only on making the chaos worse.

Panic was still spreading as people fought and struggled to avoid the danger spots. Several lay on the ground, trampled on, crushed. Ambulance men seemed to be everywhere. A fire-engine clanged past and a child toddler nearly fell beneath the wheels. A distracted woman dragged him clear.

It was unbearably hot.

A man came up to him, and said: "You all right, sir?"

"Yes." Roger recognized Hamilton, his face covered in smuts and his coat torn at the shoulder. "What about you?"

"I'm ruddy-minded," growled Hamilton, "I had the swine by his coat once. Anyway, I marked him."

Roger snapped, "How?"

"I split his lip," said Hamilton. "Look." He held up his hand, and his knuckles were bleeding. "His chin was covered in blood, I saw that much."

"Good man!" said Roger, encouraged. "We might

do something yet. Come on!" He rushed towards the loud-speaker van, which was no longer working. The driver was sitting at the wheel, a worried operator was standing by its side. The crowd was further away, now. Roger called out: "Get to the fringe of the crowd, driver. Police." He did not need to show his card, for the driver let in the clutch at once. "Where's the mike?" Roger asked.

"In the back."

"I'll go in the back," said Roger.

It was a small van, and there was only room for two of them. Hamilton was left behind, the operator crouched inside with Roger, who asked: "How does it work?"

"I've only got to switch it on."

"Switch on, will you?" said Roger.

"It's on."

Roger said: "Calling all police, calling all police. Detain all men with cut lip or cut face. Detain all men with cut lip or cut face. Calling all police . . ."

The operator tugged at his arm. He stopped speaking.

"It won't go over well while we're on the move. Better stop every twenty yards or so."

"All right," said Roger.

It was a nightmare journey. Frightened people were crushed against the sides and wheels of the van. Two men tried to climb on to it; Roger, half in and half out, pushed them off. If they broke the loud-speakers fitted on the top, the last faint chance would be gone. When he was not talking, the operator was repeating the words: "Calling all police. Calling all police. Stop all men with cut lip or cut face. Stop all men . . ."

Sweat was pouring down Roger's face.

They were able to move more freely now, for the crowd had thinned out here. They were going uphill, and when they reached the summit, the operator said: "We've been all round, once."

"Start again," said Roger.

"I've heard two other vans repeating your message," said the operator. "You ought to get your man."

"Yes. Keep at it, please," said Roger.

He was hoarse, limp, bitterly disappointed, and Henby and Cynthia were vivid in his mind's eye. Why had they come?

Now that the van could move more freely, he could look out of the back and see what had happened. Smoke was still rising from some of the fires, and he could hear other vans broadcasting the same message. He had remembered the story of the pseudo policeman and realized that a policeman in uniform would have more chance of getting through the crowd than anyone else. The trouble was that it had been too big an affair. It was impossible to watch every yard of the Heath. If it had been possible to throw a cordon round so that every man was watched——

Loud-speakers were still working on the fringes of the crowd, and he could hear first one and then the other.

Dazed and dejected people were walking about or sitting on the grass. Litter was everywhere, and black smuts seemed to darken every tree. The people looked dirty as well as dejected, and many were still frightened. Under a tree, several were stretched out on the ground with ambulance men bending over them. Mounted police had appeared and were riding round, scrutinizing everyone who passed. Roger did not attract their attention.

Then a loud-speaker van came by.

"Calling all police. Take suspects to Hampstead police station. Take suspects . . ."

"Want me to plug that?" asked the operator.

"I think I'd better get to the police station," said Roger.

The police station was five minutes' drive away. Outside a dozen cars and a large crowd of people were gathered. Men were being led in, uniformed police were being hard put to keep order. One of them spoke as Roger got out of the van.

Roger saw at least a dozen men with bruised and bleeding faces, several of them with cut lips. He laughed again, and then pulled himself together. "This won't do!" The whole business was going to his head.

Near the building, there was some order. The injured men were being put into a queue and were filing slowly into the station.

"I wish I knew O'Dare better," thought Roger.

The men on duty at the door did not recognize him, and he had to show his card. He looked at the injured men, but the great majority did not even faintly resemble O'Dare. His spirits dropped further. Two or three Scotland Yard men recognized him and spoke, but he did not stop. He went upstairs to the Superintendent's office. The door swung open, and the first voice he heard was that of Chatworth.

"Sit down, West. I've got some news for you," he said. "Plomley is dead. His body was found on the fairground and has just been identified. Murdered, as you might expect." He leaned forward and took a small packet from the desk, a packet about the size of a flat tin of fifty cigarettes, wrapped in brown paper and sealed with gummed paper. "This was in his pocket," he said. "It's just been brought in."

Roger took it without a word. It was soiled, and one corner was dented. He felt a curious sense of disappointment, as if the packet did not matter. Henby and Cynthia mattered.

"That's the one all right, sir," he said.

Roger pushed the tip of the knife beneath a strip of gummed paper. It was not easy to open and he could not keep his hands steady. Piece after piece came off, and at last the brown paper was in his hand. Inside was a small tin box; it was a flat-fifty, of pre-war manufacture.

He opened it; folded papers were inside.

There were hurried footsteps in the passage, and a man burst in. Roger recognized Sloan, still disguised, a most excited Sloan. Yet the sight of Chatworth made him stop in his tracks.

"I'm sorry, sir. I didn't know——"

"What is it?" asked Chatworth, sharply.

Sloan said: "We've got O'Dare, sir! There isn't any doubt about it, sir. He's admitted it, too. He's knocked about pretty badly, and his lip wants stitching up. He's all in, sir. He tried to get away but he couldn't summon up the strength. We've got him, sir."

Chapter Twenty-four

WHO KILLED RIDDEL?

In O'Dare's pockets were two tickets to Buenos Aires and a letter, addressed to him as Preston at an address in Hoxton. For the time being O'Dare was hardly capable of speaking, for his lip was cut so badly; stitches had been put in by a police-surgeon at Hampstead. Roger went to see him at the hospital, and asked him to write a statement. O'Dare looked up at him with bloodshot eyes in which there was a gleam of devilment. He stretched out his hand for pencil and paper, and as Roger stood over him he wrote swiftly, then flung the paper at Roger.

All he had written was: Do you know who killed Riddel. West? I didn't.

"That isn't going to get you anywhere," said Roger. "You'll have to make a full statement. Why make difficulties for yourself?"

O'Dare said nothing, but his eyes were laughing.

"We know you murdered Plomley at the Heath," Roger said. "You can't save yourself, O'Dare, but you might be able to save some of your friends."

O'Dare waved to the paper and tried to speak; the words sounded like: "Who killed Riddel, West? I didn't."

Roger said: "Do you know who did?"

O'Dare nodded.

"You know if you turn Queen's Evidence you'll get a lighter sentence, don't you?" asked Roger.

O'Dare stretched out for the pencil again, and wrote: "Do your own dirty work." Then he flung the pencil away, and lay back on his pillows and closed his eyes.

Roger went to the Hoxton address with Sloan, who had somehow managed not to get hurt. It was in a back street in the poorest quarter, and O'Dare had rented a single room. In it were several suit-cases, packed ready for the flight on the next day, and Sloan looked about him and asked whether Roger had any idea who was to be his travelling companion.

"No," said Roger. "Let's get those cases open."

All were locked, but none of the locks was difficult to pick. Roger opened his first and found it packed with O'Dare's clothes. He pulled each garment out, to search the case more thoroughly and suddenly Sloan's lock clicked open.

"Well I'm damned!" exclaimed Sloan, a moment later. "What do you make of that?"

Neatly packed were women's clothes, of excellent quality. Roger turned away from O'Dare's case to look at them. He found it difficult to take in the situation, and he fingered some silk lingerie absently. Sloan was looking at him expectantly.

"Are they Mrs Riddel's?"

"I expect so," said Roger.

"So he was going off with her, and Henby discovered it," Sloan said, his eyes bright. "Do you think that's it?"

"I wouldn't be surprised. But, of course, it might have been anybody—Mary Anson, for instance." He spoke dully.

Sloan said: "What's the trouble, Roger?"

"I don't know," said Roger. "I've a feeling that something has been put across us. Something very clever. Think of all the tricks which have been used. Those finger-prints might have hanged Henby. There might be something else just as cunning. This looks like evidence that Cynthia Riddel was planning a getaway with O'Dare, and yet——" He broke off, took out a handkerchief, and saw the initials in one corner, "C.R."

"That about settles it," said Sloan.

"Yes," said Roger, heavily. "Well, let's see what else we can find."

The cases held nothing except clothes, Treasury notes in small denominations and a few odds and ends of no importance. But a thorough search of the rooms brought to light files of papers, account books and record books, hidden under the floor-boards. There was something else; a small incendiary bomb of the petrol type; once exploded, it would have reduced the contents of the room to ashes in a few moments.

"Well, we now know how the fire was started on the Heath," said Sloan. "What are you going to do with this stuff?"

"Take it to the Yard," said Roger.

When he reached Scotland Yard, a little after six o'clock, he found Mark waiting for him disconsolately. Eddie Day was also there. Chatworth had just gone out, he said, but Eddie was to tell Roger that he would be back after seven o'clock, and hoped a full statement would be ready.

"And believe me, he meant it," said Eddie, with relish. "He's on the warpath, Roger, you'd better not slip up on this business. Do you know what?"

"What?"

"Plomley and Chatworth were at school together. And the Varsity," breathed Eddie. "No wonder he's been snooty over this, 'Andsome. You'd better look out."

"I don't think we need worry about that," said Roger. "It explains why Chatworth has been a bit touchy, that's all. Do you know if Tandy or any of the others have talked yet?"

"Chatworth said they were to be left to you."

"Kind of him," said Roger, and looked at Mark. "Any news of Henby and Mrs Riddel?"

"Henby's not badly hurt," said Mark. "He's been sent home, and Ingleton is looking after him. Mrs Riddel is still in hospital. She's badly burned about the legs, and her face suffered a bit. I gathered that there's no fear of her dying and not much fear of her face being disfigured."

"Oh," said Roger, and added under his breath: "That's a pity."

"What's that?" asked Mark.

"It doesn't matter," said Roger. "I'm sorry, old chap, but I'll have to go through these papers on my own; it will be more than Chatworth would stand if you were to go through them with me. Will you go home and keep Janet company?"

"Er—yes," said Mark. He hesitated, and Roger went with him to the door. "What's on your mind, Roger?"

"Cynthia Riddel and Henby," admitted Roger. "I hope to know something more about it when I've been through this stuff. I'll let you know the result as soon as I can."

"Right-ho," said Mark.

Then Sloan and Abbott came in, and went through the papers with Roger. At first there was no sound in the office but the rustle of the papers. Then Eddie Day went out, saying breezily that he was glad it wasn't his job. After that, Sloan and Roger kept looking at each other, the light of understanding in their eyes. Even Abbott exclaimed aloud from time to time as they all compared notes. They finished a little after seven o'clock, except for the flat packet. Abbott had it, and after a moment's hesitation he passed it to Roger and said:

"I think you'd better open this, West."

"Thanks," said Roger. "We know pretty well what's in it, though."

"We think we do," said Abbott.

As Roger opened the packet, he thought of the evidence which had already been found. It was overwhelming proof against Plomley. He had defrauded the Government frequently, with the help of one or two prominent permanent officials. The facts revealed a scandal of such proportions that as soon as a Government inquiry into his interests was mentioned, Plomley must have known that the end was near unless he could cover up the traces of the frauds.

At long last, Roger took out the papers in the box. He unfolded them one by one and glanced through them, then passed them on to the others. The first papers summarized the statements and accounts in the Hoxton room. Then one, found at the bottom, made Roger open his eyes wide. It outlined the plans which Plomley had made to cover up the traces of his dishonesty, plans which would have succeeded in a few months. The work had already been begun; falsified statements and accounts were being filed in place of the real ones in the Government departments concerned. The gravity of the situation could hardly be exaggerated.

"But he was getting away with it," said Sloan in bewilderment. "He would probably have succeeded. The select committee wouldn't have found anything against him."

"Someone did, and that someone blackmailed him," said Abbott. "O'Dare, of course. Perhaps there was someone else—do you think so, West?"

"Yes," said Roger.

"But why were attacks made on the members of the committee?" demanded Sloan. "It doesn't make sense. Plomley had his plans already set, his game surely was to let the committee carry on. I can't make it out. I just can't make it out."

"I think I'll see Tandy and the others," said Roger.

He went outside, as the prisoners were in Cannon Row police station. He was glad of a few minutes in the fresh air, and stood smoking a cigarette when Chatworth drove into the Yard. Chatworth pulled up, and asked what news there was. Roger reported formally. Chatworth nodded, and then said exactly the same as Sloan; there seemed no sense in Riddel's murder.

"I'm hoping I'll get something from Tandy now, sir," said Roger. "If not, then we'll have to try O'Dare again. I found evidence, at Hoxton, that he spent some years in a circus as an acrobat, which explains his agility. Then he settled down, developed his interest in chemistry, and joined Plomley. He maintained his associations with the circus people, especially with Tandy and the others. Tandy, it proves, was the leader of a racecourse gang which spread its activities pretty widely. O'Dare was the directing genius and took a quarter of the profits. There were one or two deaths during race-gang fights, Tandy committed at least one murder. The whole gang was implicated, and as far as I can see—and Superintendent Abbott agrees, sir—O'Dare had got these people exactly where he wanted them. They did whatever he told them. What I don't yet know is how he managed to make them keep their mouths shut over this business."

"Go and see them," said Chatworth, abruptly.

Roger expected to find Tandy and all the others as silent and sullen as ever, but as he passed Tandy's cell the man called eagerly:

"West! West, I've something to tell you."

The sergeant came up and opened the barred door, and Roger went in. Tandy, unshaven and in need of a hair-cut, looked at him tensely, and demanded:

"Is it true that Plomley's dead and you've got O'Dare?"

"Yes," said Roger. "It's in the evening papers, and that ought to convince you. Have you an Evening News?" he called out to the sergeant.

"Yes, sir, coming."

"Never mind that," said Tandy. "I'll take your word for it, West. So Plomley's dead. O'Dare always told us that Plomley could do what he liked with the Assistant Commissioner and the Home Secretary." He was talking so fast that Roger had difficulty in understanding him. "He said all we had to do was to keep our mouths shut and we'd be all right." He broke off, and Roger saw the fear in the man's eyes, the fear of coming trial and punishment. But in those few words he had explained the whole reason for his silence and that of his friends. O'Dare had convinced him that while Plomley was alive, they were clear and they had taken that for gospel.

"Go on," said Roger.

Tandy said: "You know O'Dare was putting the black on Plomley, don't you?"

"Yes. What I don't know is why O'Dare killed Riddel."

Tandy said: "O'Dare didn't kill Riddel!"

"Then who did?"

"I dunno," said Tandy, "but O'Dare knows all right. I can tell you plenty about the rest of the game. Is it Queen's Evidence? Will you see me through?"

"I'll do what I can for you," said Roger slowly.

"I know you will, West, you're a good guy," declared Tandy eagerly. "You remember the day you first saw me, West, and I took that packet off you? Bray had gone to get it out of Henby's room—O'Dare knew Henby had it. When Bray fell down on the job I hung around, I couldn't believe my eyes when I saw it in your hand. It was just a gift to me."

Roger said sharply: "Are you telling the truth?"

'Why, yes! Ask any of the others. They'll talk now

they know Plomley's dead and you've got O'Dare. Henby had that packet all right."

Roger looked at him levelly, and in his heart he believed the man. He hesitated for a few minutes, and then went on:

"I see, Tandy. You shot Marriott, didn't you?"

"O'Dare made me," protested Tandy, "he'd been putting the black on me for years. I didn't have no choice, West."

"That may be true," admitted Roger. "Well, what else?"

"I don't know much else," said Tandy, "but I can tell you this. O'Dare was sweet on the Riddel woman at one time. She turned him down flat. After that O'Dare hated her and her old man and Henby like Hitler hated Jews. That's true, too. He always boasted he'd get her in the end."

"Oh," said Roger, blankly.

There was little else to be learned from Tandy, and the others said no more than confirm what Tandy had told him.

Roger went across to the Yard, and reported. Chatworth listened without comment, and then said:

"So Henby had the packet. It looks as if he was in it with O'Dare, doesn't it?"

"And they fell out," said Roger. "Yes, I suppose it does. I'll go and see Henby at once, sir."

"Take Sloan with you," said Chatworth.

Henby was sitting up in bed in his own flat, and Ingleton was with him. Ingleton protested that Henby was in no condition to be questioned, but Henby, his head bandaged, laughed and told him not to be a fool. Henby was certainly in good spirits. Ingleton went out, and Henby said abruptly:

"O'Dare sent me a message to see him and Ireland at Hampstead—the Well Street place, West—and Ingleton subbed for me. He went only as a messenger. I hope you haven't got any queer idea that he's mixed up in this?"

"I'm not worried about Ingleton at the moment," said Roger. "When did you get that packet, Henby? Bray came here to steal it, not plant it."

There was a long, strained silence. Henby's mood changed, his mouth was tightly closed, and he was gripping the sheets in front of him. He did not look frightened, but he frowned. The blow had hit him hard, thought Roger; perhaps he now realized that all hope was gone. At last Henby moved, and said harshly:

"I see. So O'Dare talked."

"His men have. You lied to me about the packet. You've lied to me about other things. You and O'Dare between you were blackmailing Plomley——"

"What?" cried Henby.

"And nothing will help you now," concluded Roger.

"If you'll believe that you'll believe anything," snapped Henby. "Riddel was the blackmailer, surely you knew that."

Roger thought. "Of course: *Riddel* blackmailed Plomley."

Henby had always tried to shield Cynthia, too: against her husband.

"Did Mrs Riddel know?" Roger asked, quietly.

"She learned of it, but if you're thinking that she killed Riddel, you're quite wrong. She married Riddel because she knew that disclosures would be made about Plomley if she refused. She thought that with marriage she would put an end to it all, but——"

Roger interrupted: "In O'Dare's rooms we found a case of Mrs Riddel's clothes. She was going to fly abroad with him. You learned that and followed her to Hampstead, didn't you? Isn't that a strong enough reason to stop defending her, and to tell the truth?"

"I am telling the truth," insisted Henby. "That case

of clothes was stolen. O'Dare sent for her, and told her she could see her father at the tent. She knew she had promised you to stay at Grosvenor Place, but she felt she must see Plomley. I knew there was danger and went with her. I don't doubt that O'Dare planned to take her away, and thought he could if he put the screw on Plomley once more. But she would never have gone with him. When we got there, O'Dare boasted of the money he had already collected that day. He actually showed us some, and told us how he'd worked it. Then he said that Plomley was in the rear part of the tent. He taunted Cynthia to breaking point; I could have killed him where he sat. He said that he wanted one more thing before he would stop blackmailing Plomley. I didn't know what he meant then. I know now——" Henby's voice was harsh. "He was about to explain when the telephone rang—he had a telephone there. He listened, jumped up and snapped: 'West's coming, I'll teach you to lead him here.' And— then came the explosion and the fire. I saw him dash out of the tent, but I had my work cut out to get Cynthia away."

Henby stopped, and looked intently at Roger. The room was quiet for a long time.

"I see," said Roger, at last. "Let's get back to the sealed case. Where did you get it?"

"Cynthia had it."

"You mean Mrs Riddel took it after she killed her husband?"

After another long pause, Henby said: "West, Cynthia did not kill Riddel. She found an unfinished letter to you in his pocket, thought then he had given the sealed packet to you for safe custody, and came to see you. After her first visit, she found it locked in his desk. She brought it to me, and I put it where I thought it was safe. After-wards she visited you again, with the dummy packet. But she did not kill Riddel."

"According to the available evidence, she was out of London when Riddel was killed," admitted Roger. "But I do not believe that now."

Henby said flatly: "It happens to be true."

"All right!" Roger turned on his heel. "I didn't want to question her in the state she is in to-night, but there's no choice. Come on, Bill." He moved with Sloan towards the door.

Henby watched them until the door was open and Sloan was outside.

Then: "West!" called Henby, with a desperate note in his voice.

Roger turned: "Well?"

"Cynthia was in London when Riddel was murdered," said Henby. "She came here afterwards and I hid her. She and her father had been trying to make Riddel show some mercy. Riddel simply gloated and Plomley killed him. Immediately afterwards O'Dare came in."

The whole case was clear enough now, Roger said to Mark and Janet, late that night. O'Dare in a very different mood, had admitted arriving just after Plomley had killed Riddel. O'Dare himself had mutilated Riddel's face, to make it look a different type of crime and, with the added influence over Plomley, had blackmailed him to a pitch which seemed to have no limits. Henby——

"He must love her very much," said Janet, very quietly.

"He's come near to ruining his career because of her," said Roger, "but I think it will work out all right."

"But why was Garner murdered?" Mark asked.

"I've got the truth of that from O'Dare," said Roger. "Garner had an idea of what Plomley had done, Plomley discovered this, and told O'Dare. O'Dare planned Garner's murder and very nearly succeeded in framing Henby. O'Dare had always wanted Cynthia Plomley, and lost her to Riddel. After Riddel's death, he realized that with Henby in the running he had no chance. The man wasn't—isn't—sane, of course. By the way, he wanted Mary Anson to act as a go-between. That's why he sent for her from Well Street. Nice case, wasn't it?"

"It was a hateful case," said Janet, feelingly. "Still, it has brought Mrs Riddel and Henby together at last, and even perhaps——" she looked at Mark and laughed— "turned our Benedict into a Romeo! Will Cynthia be disfigured, Roger?"

"No," said Roger. "I saw a report from the hospital just before I left the Yard." He smiled. "I think I'd better telephone Henby and tell him that, don't you?"